# The Fabulist

# The Fabulist

## Chris Bedell

BLKDOG

www.blkdogpublishing.com

# Other titles by Chris Bedell

*Burning Bridges*

*Cousin Dearest*

*I Know Where the Bodies are Buried*

# Chapter 1

Good girls killed out of necessity, not choice.

The idea was true even if it sounded obvious. It was a concept that came up in my Philosophy class at one point. I couldn't disagree, though, as most people didn't wake up wanting to be killers. They just found themselves thrown into bad situations, which was beginning to hit too close to home at the moment.

I emptied the contents of the canister onto the body, not even bothering to blink at the stench of gasoline or the corpse.

Elena paced back and forth, ruffling the leaves with her high heels. "We shouldn't be doing this. We can still go to my mom."

Robbie snickered. "Doubtful. We're in deep shit as it is."

I ran my fingers through my hair, tucking a lock behind my ear. "We don't have a choice. Besides, you're my friends. You're supposed to help me."

Dylan stood there with his pushed back, brown hair, and if the situation weren't so tragic, I would've laughed. He was never one to keep quiet because he would've made his opinion known under any other situation. But not this one. There was no good way to spin being an accomplice to murder.

Chuck smiled. "Of course. You know we're here for you. Whatever you need."

"That's easy for you to say," Robbie said. "You're only part of our group because you're sleeping with Cassandra."

Chuck remained silent, rolling his eyes. I couldn't blame him since I would've slapped Robbie across the face if I didn't have more important things to worry about.

Knowing Chuck supported me was something to hold onto, though—even if it wouldn't erase my problems. I didn't know what I would've done if nobody saw a shred of humanity in me.

I struck a match, dropping it on the body before a sea of red, orange, and yellow engulfed the corpse.

Elena picked at her nail, causing part of it to peel off. "I hope you're happy."

It wasn't long before the smell of burnt flesh hit my nose. I rubbed the side of my head. It didn't do any good. More tears fell down my face without warning. Like I said, just because I had to do this, didn't mean I wanted to.

Robbie crossed his arms. "You could've gone to the police, Cassandra. Last time I checked, blackmail is a crime."

I almost choked on a gulp of my own air. "Are you kidding me, Robbie? Have you forgotten fraud is also a crime?"

"Then maybe you shouldn't have come up with such a convoluted lie." Robbie pushed his sleeves up. "Besides, don't pretend to be a good person. You're nothing but a self-righteous bitch. After all, I'm sure Lucy was thrilled to be on her own for a year."

Robbie didn't have to be asshole. I stood by Robbie when I found out he was bisexual and never judged him. Even if he paid too much attention to his wardrobe when nobody was looking.

An owl hooted, sending chills up my back. The outdoors had never been my thing, and I wouldn't change my mind anytime soon. There was something unnerving about leaving the comfort of the indoors behind for an unpredictable world.

"In case you've forgotten, there was a reason for me coming up with the lie in the first place. But I guess you don't care." I paused, struggling to take a breath. "But you know what? You're the one who chose to help me. So, that says more about you, not me."

The vein surfaced on Robbie's head, almost popping. "Are you really gonna stand there and give me that bullshit?"

Liar.

I wasn't an idiot. I knew what people called me behind my back when they thought I wasn't listening. It was still better than being called a sociopath, though, because it wasn't like I wanted to hurt anyone. I just couldn't help myself. Dishonesty was an addiction, meaning lying was to me like what gambling and drugs were for some people.

Robbie shot Elena a glance. "What happened to you? You were the one who originally agreed with me in the first place."

Elena averted her gaze, staring at a squirrel climbing up a tree. "It wouldn't do any good now."

I scurried towards Robbie while the mixture of his earthly and sweet cologne wafted through the air. "I'm done arguing with you, Robbie. You need to get with the program ASAP."

Dylan lifted his gaze, giving me a brief glance. "What about the murder weapon? We should get rid of it, don't you think?"

"I already took care of that. The weapon is on his person." I tugged at the sides of my jacket.

Elena shook her head. "Have you lost your damn mind?"

I wagged my index finger at her. "Get your mind out of the gutter. I put it in his jacket pocket."

"Oh." Elena sucked on her teeth.

It was good I wasn't the only who was still surprised by things. But if Elena thought I put the murder weapon in a certain spot, then she was even more demented than me.

The wind whistled, causing my hair to bounce around while an awkward silence ensued. This shouldn't have been my life. I was 17. I should have been worried about sneaking out past curfew or drinking when no one was looking, not covering up a murder.

I glanced at everyone. "Do we all agree? Nobody is gonna say anything? This is our little secret?"

They nodded their heads within a couple of seconds.

Wonderful. At least we still agreed about something, not that it provided me with much comfort or anything. My problems would still be there in the morning. I knew it, and they knew it.

But I'd pray the rest of the world would never find out what happened. It'd be our undoing, and that was one disaster I didn't want to see. It wasn't something I wanted—even if I might have enjoyed hearing about turbulent celebrity lifestyles as much as the next person

That fact was, I had enough monsters to deal with at the moment.

Okay, that wasn't a 100 percent true. There was something intoxicating about being the center of attention even though stress still existed, which was something I'd consider no matter how appealing the spotlight was.

* * *

The "murder" was a story for another day, though.

For now, it was the last week of August.

I was still, "Kidnapped Girl," and had two months before I'd turn into, "Murder Girl," which meant I still had to be "found." And when I was discovered, I'd give the performance of a century.

I'd probably resurface sooner rather than later, though. Especially given the identity of the dead man plastered on the headline from the newspaper I currently gripped while I sat in a chair by a desk, as the blinds remained closed and sweat dripped down my face.

Although one fact remained clear. There was always a hint of truth in the biggest lie, and the only question was whether people would believe me.

# Chapter 2

I exited the convenience store, attempting to ignore the beaming sun while biting my lip. Summer was better than winter even if the heat was annoying.

The carbonation from the soda fell into my mouth, pricking my throat. Two people—who were several feet away from me—stopped walking.

The first person gasped. "Fuck! That's Cassandra Jenkins."

"Yeah, it is," said the second person.

In retrospect, I should've had more than sunglasses on. I should've also sported my red wig. It was part of my Katrina Venus alias. I even had a fake I.D. to go along with the disguise.

***

I sat in an interview room at the police station in my hometown of Clarksville a couple of hours after being spotted. My jaw twitched even though I usually never got nervous. I just couldn't help myself since everything had to go right.

The door opened, revealing a female with a badge attached to her belt. The overhead light even glinted against the badge, accentuating its gold texture.

She strutted over to the table, then sat down across from me. After that, she forced a smile. "I'm Detective Jane Sanders. I've been working your abduction case for the last year. It must be a relief to be home?"

Abduction.

I guess I should back up to when I "allegedly" went missing a year ago after going out for a jog in my neighborhood.

I remained silent, resisting the urge to bite my nails—I wasn't a little kid anymore. Acting my age should've at least been attempted.

I inhaled a deep breath. "Am I in trouble?"

She leaned closer, sliding her elbows up the table. "No. Of course not. Why would you ask that?"

A lump lingered in my throat, and I couldn't swallow it. "I don't know. Bad a habit I guess."

Jane's eyebrows rose. "Can you tell me anything about the last year? I can't imagine what it must have felt like to be kidnapped."

I shook my head. "No. Not particularly."

I gazed at her while my pulse rang in my ears. I could only begin to speculate about the judgments forming in her head.

She coughed. "I don't mean to sound blunt, but you look well for someone who has been held captive for a year."

A burning sensation jabbed my stomach. Damn. I'd have to be careful with this detective—counting on her stupidity would've been foolish. "Thank you," I said.

"If you don't mind me asking, do you know what you were doing in Jamesfield?" Jane asked. "It isn't that I think you're lying, but why would your abductor even let out you in the real world?"

I tapped my feet against the tile floor. "We were gonna visit one of his friends in Virginia. I begged for a soda because I was thirsty and offered to sleep with him if he granted me this kindness."

"There's something else you should know. I'm not trying to overwhelm you, but your father died."

I didn't even flinch or cry. Good riddance. The world was better off because nobody else knew him like I did.

She plucked a loose eyelash. "Don't you wanna know how your dad died?"

I focused my attention on my right wrist, choosing not to make eye contact with the detective. "No. But I bet you're gonna tell me anyway."

Jane coughed into her right arm. "He died in a fire. Your house burned to the ground. Although your sister, Lucy, survived."

I feigned a smile. "That's great."

"She's living with your friend Elena's mom. She was granted temporary guardianship by the court until a more permanent solution arises." Her eyes widened. "How'd you get that scar?"

I sighed. "I was cooking. I accidentally forgot to turn the stove off and placed my wrist on the burner."

Detective Sanders frowned. "That seems to be a big scar for such a wound."

I gritted my teeth. "Are you calling me a liar?"

"No. Of course not. I'd never blame the victim. You can ask any of my colleagues if you don't believe me."

No one could ever discover how I got the scar—it was a secret I'd take to my grave. It wasn't like anyone would believe me if I told the truth. That was the problem with always lying. When I finally had a shred of honesty, nobody would be around to help me.

A woman burst through the door, and ran towards me. I would've recognized the brunette hair anywhere. It was Elena's mother.

She grinned at me. "It's so good to see you, Cassandra."

I nodded. "Same. You don't know how good it feels to be home."

I stood, then shuffled towards Mrs. Brooks. She opened her arms, inviting me in for a hug. She patted my back while I sobbed because my current emotional state was the one thing I didn't have to fake.

I pulled back from the embrace after a beat.

She put her hands in her pockets. "I don't know if you know, but your father died."

I nodded. "Detective Sanders told me everything. How's Lucy holding up?"

"As well as can be expected." She rubbed the side of her eye. "She's still in school, as is Elena. We can tell them about you when they come home in the afternoon."

"Sounds good," I said.

Mrs. Brooks tilted her head in the detective's direction. "Can she leave?"

"Yeah, but I want you to know I'll be conducting more interviews." Detective Sanders brushed the dust off her blazer. She must've been somebody to always worry about appearances. I couldn't blame her even if I found her questions annoying, though. I also prided myself with superficial things like beauty.

Appearances were everything even if people didn't want to admit it. It was a fact of life. Snapped judgments happened all the time. The sooner people realized that, the better off they'd be.

Mrs. Brooks grimaced. "Of course."

It appeared I wasn't the only person who wasn't crazy about Detective Sanders—I'd bet my life on how Mrs. Brooks must've thought it was inappropriate to badger us about a follow-up interview. I was kidnapped for the last year, and was supposed to be thinking about getting readjusted to society. Not having the police on my ass.

I would have to be more careful. Being away from

the outside world didn't do me any good because I must've forgotten how to act around normal people. Deception was supposed to be calculating and covert. If I had to tell people what they wanted to hear to appease them, then so be it. I was a master manipulator. That was what happened when my life became about surviving and not living.

I didn't talk to Mrs. Brooks on the car ride back to her house since my eyes remained fixated on the view from the window. The mixture of red, orange, and red leaves popped out at me while each landscape rolled into the next. There was no denying it. Fall was coming even if it was still the last week of August.

* * *

Mrs. Brooks allowed my friends Robbie and Dylan to come over for a couple of hours after we talked to Elena and Lucy when they returned from school.

The four of us were in my new bedroom at the moment a.k.a. one of Elena's extra guest rooms. I'd concede it. Elena's big house was a good thing. It meant I didn't have to share a bedroom with my sister. And I'd relish the victory even if it were a small one.

Elena was still grinning. The novelty must not have worn off yet. But then again, it wasn't every day that a kidnapped best friend resurfaced. It was one for the ages.

"Are you ever gonna stop smiling, Elena?" I asked.

Her cheeks turned brighter than the red on Santa's suit. "I can't help it. You don't know how worried we all were, weren't we?"

Elena's gaze drifted to Robbie and Dylan. Wow. It was time for the heavy pressure.

Robbie sucked in a breath. "Elena's right."

"What Robbie said," Dylan replied.

I twirled a strand of my blonde hair. "Have you found a boyfriend yet, Robbie?"

"No." He paused for a beat. "What can I say? Not

that many kids are out at the high school."

I rolled my eyes at him. "You're bisexual."

Robbie took a moment to respond. If I didn't know better, he must've been counting to ten under his breath. My comment could've been viewed as offensive, and he must have wanted to smack me across my face after it. "Same difference," Robbie said.

I glanced at Elena. "How's Lucy been?"

"Okay, I guess. But I'm not gonna lie. The last year was hard on her. Hell, it was difficult on all of us. We didn't know if you were alive or dead in a ditch somewhere." Elena's jaw trembled.

I cackled. The sound of my voice echoed through the entire bedroom, lingering in the air for a moment. It was almost enough to prick the hairs on my back. "No need to be melodramatic."

Elena glared at me. "Are you really gonna lecture me?"

She had a point. This wasn't a plot out of some lame Hollywood movie. My kidnapping was "real." I might not have talked on the ride home, but Mrs. Brooks did. There were MISSING posters of me everywhere. Impossible to go one block without seeing a MISSING poster of me. It was amazing, really. I hadn't even had to put any energy into being the center of attention—everything fell into place without any effort. It was beautiful.

I grinned. "But please, Elena. Tell your mom that I appreciate her buying me an entire new wardrobe."

Elena clipped over to the bed, giving me a pat on the back before sitting down. "Of course. But don't worry. My mom is more understanding than you can imagine since you lost everything in the fire."

Robbie's shoulders tensed. "You had time to buy new clothes?"

"It wasn't my idea," I said.

* * *

I descended the staircase the following morning around 5:45 A.M., making my way into the kitchen. Mrs. Brooks was already there. If she hadn't told me her husband was away on a business conference, I would've been surprised he wasn't right there with his wife in the kitchen. Or worse. I would've thought there were marital problems between the two of them. I whipped my head back and forth. I couldn't be so mean because Mrs. Brooks opened her home to Lucy and me when we had no place else to go.

"Can I make you anything for breakfast?" Mrs. Brooks said. "Also, there's something else I wanted to talk to you about."

I lifted my eyebrows at her. "What's up?"

She tugged at her pearl necklace, wrapping it around her fingers. "Are you sure you wanna go back to school today? Nobody would think less of you if you took the rest of the week off. This isn't a race."

"No. I'm good. I just want to immerse myself in my old life. Is that okay with you?"

Mrs. Brooks nodded. "How do you want to get to school? Elena or Lucy could drive you if you want. They each have their own cars. Or I could take you if that'd be better. My boss understands I'm gonna be busy for the next few weeks."

Driving. It was an interesting idea to think about. It was something I missed out on since I only had my permit and being kidnapped prevented me from getting my license.

I allowed the matter to simmer in my mind for a few moments before opening my mouth. "Elena can drive me."

"Sounds like a plan." Mrs. Brooks reached for her mug, then chugged the rest of her coffee. Not that she needed anymore. She was already talking a mile a minute.

Maybe I shouldn't have complained, though. It

was good to know people cared—it was more than I could say about the past.

She placed the mug in the sink, then whirled around. "Was it weird being without your twin sister for a year?"

It was another thing I somehow forgot about. Lucy and I weren't just sisters. We were identical twins. Not that telling Lucy and I apart was difficult. She always had wavy hair and I had straight hair, which was almost laughable. Lucy was the calm one and I was the wild one. I smirked. There was another way to look at it. Double trouble. Although if I were being 100 percent honest, I was double trouble for the both of us—Lucy didn't have it in her to be as theatrical as me.

* * *

Elena and I left before Lucy, and I shuffled through the school hallway half an hour later. Lucy must've been in one of her moods or something. It was understandable. It wasn't easy to compete with someone like me. I outshined even the most obnoxious person. It wasn't a secret; the entire world knew it.

I told Elena I wanted to go to the guidance counselor's office on my own—I wouldn't have had it any other way. Acting normal was the only thing that mattered.

I turned the corner in the hallway, not even noticing I was getting lost in my own thoughts before bumping into somebody.

Textbooks smacked against the floor. The guy kneeled, then picked them up in a matter of seconds.

"Sorry. I should've been paying attention," he said.

I snickered. "Don't worry about it. How come the textbooks aren't in your backpack, though? Maybe then you wouldn't have to worry about dropping them?"

"My backpack is full as it is. I am taking five AP

classes. But you can check if you don't believe me."

"I'll take your word for it." I licked my lips.

Wow. He hadn't gasped at my presence. It wasn't a narcissistic thing. It was the truth. I was the town's local celebrity. It was the only good thing that happened from being kidnapped. In fact, the news was already chatting about my reappearance.

"Is something wrong?" he asked.

The uneasy feeling lingered in my throat. "I'll be honest with you. Why aren't gawking at me? I've been kidnapped for the last year."

He sneered, revealing flared nostrils. "I'm sorry I didn't boost your ego. This is my first day in school. I moved to town last weekend."

"Sorry. How presumptuous of me." I leaned closer, then pulled his jacket collar.

"Don't worry about it." He brushed my hands off him.

The guy strutted down the hallway in the opposite direction without another word.

"Could I at least get a name?" I asked.

He spun around. "I'm Chuck."

I raised my eyes at him. "I'm Cassandra. I guess I'll see you around sometime."

Chuck bit his lip. "If you're lucky."

If Lucy or friends pulled that bullshit with me, I would've been annoyed. But not him. This time was different. It was as intoxicating as being in the spotlight or lying. He wasn't afraid to tell me what he thought. I couldn't explain it. There was just something nice about a guy not being afraid to match me blow for blow.

* * *

My father's funeral occurred the following Saturday, and Mrs. Brooks, Elena, Robbie, Dylan, and I now stood on the sidewalk in front of the church waiting for Lucy. She ended up being in another mood. It wasn't anything to worry about, though. I had 99 problems, and my sister wasn't going to be another one.

A town car pulled up to the curb before Lucy exited the front passenger seat, making her way over to us. I had to give her one thing. She had style even if it was silly she didn't take her own car.

I turned to everyone else. "I've got this. Could you guys go inside and mingle with the guests?"

Elena squeezed my hand. "Of course."

Elena guided them into the church, leaving Lucy and me to ourselves.

I forced a smile. "How are you, Lucy?"

"Fine." She glared into my eyes. "But don't pretend to care."

"And what's that supposed to mean?"

Lucy scoffed. "Everyone else might be buying your kidnapping story. But I'm not."

I furrowed an eyebrow. "Are you saying I'm lying?"

"You did, I didn't." Lucy chuckled. "But a little piece of advice, I'd be sure to get your stories straight. And yes, adding the 's' was intentional. You wouldn't want to get caught in a lie, would you?"

I scanned her body, deciding to admire her black blouse and strapless dress. At least she had good fashion sense. I might not have been able to see the label from where I stood, but nine out of ten times, I recognized Gucci anywhere. It was another one of my gifts like telling a good lie and being the center of attention.

"Let's go inside, Lucy. The sooner we go, the sooner it'll all be over." I took a cloth from my purse, wiping my eyes.

Her pupils dilated. "You can stop pretending to be sad. Nobody is watching you right now."

"I know." I clenched my jaw, as if giving myself a minor distraction would be some miraculous thing.

Lucy stepped forward. "In case you didn't realize, you and I are the only ones who know the truth about our father. Don't tell me you forgot how you got the scar on your left wrist?"

"Trust me," I said, swallowing the uneasy feeling in my throat. "Being burned with a cigarette is something I won't forget."

"Good." Lucy smiled, allowing the rest of the world to see her well-aligned teeth. Even if she always complained about how she had braces an extra year than anyone in our grade. "I'd hate to think you completely forgot about the past."

"You don't have to dredge up old memories."

"It has nothing to do with me," Lucy said. "Whether you like it or not, the past always crawls back up to the surface when you least expect it. The only question is whether you'll be ready to deal with it."

Something plopped to the ground, making a splashing sound. I looked up at the sky. Clouds remained stacked together. I guess I couldn't have been surprised it was raining. It was kind of hilarious in a morbid way.

* * *

I distracted myself that night by going through the mail even if it was unlikely I would've gotten any mail in my new home. I hadn't even been living in Elena's house for a week yet.

A letter soon stole my attention. The letter was addressed to me. I opened the envelope, yanking the contents out of it. I glanced down at the letter:

> **You might have the rest of the world wrapped around your finger with your kidnapping story. But not me! I see through the bullshit and know the whole story, and soon the rest of the world will too.**

I didn't even bother picking up the letter when it fell from my hand, yet I glanced back at the envelope on the counter. There was no return address. I couldn't say I was surprised. I thought back to Lucy's confrontation at the memorial service. She hinted about claiming to know the truth. But she couldn't have done it. Lucy wasn't that evil.

Although I'd been gone for a year.

It didn't take a genius to realize a lot could happen over the course of a year. The people I knew best were the most capable of betrayal. The theme was from my freshman English class. Even if we were just discussing books, the idea was still relevant in real life. I knew better than anyone else what it was like to cover malice with a smile.

Lucy was my twin sister, which meant we were family. She couldn't intentionally want to hurt me—she just couldn't. I shook my head, and it wasn't long before someone tapped my back. I turned around. Nobody was there.

My behavior must've been an overreaction. It had to be since the implications of living in the same house with someone as diabolical/even more evil than me were maddening.

At the very least, it was something to consider.

I would forget the matter for the moment. There were more positive things to focus on. Like Chuck.

It was nice. If I had my way, I would procure him as my next boyfriend. I did have a weakness for blonds after all. Not that I would date him for his hair color. It was just an added bonus.

Thinking about Chuck wasn't as comforting as it should have been. Blond bombshell wasn't that far of a leap from the idea of blonds in general.

And I wasn't thinking about blond bombshell as a compliment. This was great! There was no escaping it. My sister was an enemy no matter what ideas came into my mind.

I couldn't confront her, though. It had nothing to do with being afraid. If I learned anything from the last year, it was two things. Revealing that I knew what my enemy was up to was a bad idea, and people also didn't strike till their enemy was most vulnerable. The only good thing was I wasn't there yet. Nope. I still had time.

I only hoped Lucy didn't believe in another theme from one of my classes, which was good girls killed out of necessity, not choice. Because I did, and that would've meant Lucy and I were more alike than I admitted. Then again, Lucy and I shared the same past. Our father.

# Chapter 3

L ucy entered the kitchen several minutes after I dropped the letter on the floor. Then, she furrowed her eyebrows "Everything okay, Cassandra?"

I gasped, not even bothering to respond. The sketchy impression I now had of my sister remained etched in my mind. I wouldn't be forgetting it anytime soon. I couldn't. She called me a liar to my face. I didn't know what was worse. Calling me a liar to my face or behind my back. Confronting me didn't make her a better person. It just made her ballsy, and I'd give her points for that. But there was still the feeling of a fly buzzing around my face before swatting it.

"Yeah, I'm fine. I couldn't be better," I said.

Her gaze shifted to the floor. "You dropped something."

Beads of sweat clung to my face. "It's nothing. You really should learn to mind your own business."

I didn't wait for her to pick up the note. I kneeled down on the ground, grabbing it before plopping back up and shoving the note back into my pocket.

Lucy put her hands on her hips. "It doesn't look like nothing."

I crossed my arms. "Shouldn't you be in bed?"

Her teeth poked her lip. "Maybe you lost track of the days because of being kidnapped, but it isn't a school night. It's Saturday. Besides, you should lighten up."

"Wow. And I thought I was arrogant," I said.

"I came into the kitchen to get a glass of water." She paused for a moment. "Not that it's any of your business."

Lucy shuffled over to the cabinet, then pulled out a glass from the top shelf. She yanked the faucet to the left, allowing the water to ooze into the cup. Lucy gulped down the water in a matter of seconds. Wow. She must've really been parched.

I stared at the floor, making sure not to make eye contact with her. "It shouldn't be like this, Lucy. We're sisters."

"Then maybe you should start taking that seriously."

Shit. I should've looked her in the eye if I wanted her to believe me.

"If you have a problem with me, then tell me," I said.

Lucy snickered. "I did, Cassandra. But maybe you're too thick to realize it. In case you haven't noticed, I'm not playing weak anymore."

Lucy didn't wait for me to respond. She just strutted out of the kitchen without another word. If I had any doubts about her sending the note before, they were gone. Lucy must've sent the note. It was kind of genius. She lived at the same house, and would only have to walk less than a 1000 steps to the mailbox, which wouldn't require any effort.

The thought of her blackmailing me left a bitter feeling, though. Worse than a child being forced to eat vegetables.

Wait.

I couldn't call it blackmail. The person didn't state a demand. It was only a twisted game. That was all it was. Whether the conflict would escalate or not remained to be seen. There was no denying it. I would have to be more careful around Lucy.

* * *

Robbie and I hung out in my bedroom the following Monday after school to organize my closet. It didn't matter if fashion was a stereotype of bisexual/gay guys. Every girl needed a bisexual or gay friend. It was like being friends with a girl without the bitchiness. I didn't even need to see the movie *GBF* to realize that.

"What do you want me to do with this dress?" Robbie asked.

I pointed to the closet. "It's kind of formal. You can just hang it up because I can't imagine wearing it at the moment."

"Okay. Cool." Robbie walked over to the closet, then grabbed a hanger. It wasn't long before he hung up the dress.

"How's everything going with you? I take it Dylan still doesn't know the truth?" I asked.

His cheeks turned pale, replacing his normal fair skin. "If it's okay with you, I don't wanna discuss it."

Maybe it was a mistake to mention Dylan. But it wasn't like I wanted to hurt Robbie. I was making conversation—it was what friends did. If people couldn't talk about romantic prospects with their best friends, then the world must have been coming to an end. Wow. Look at me! Another dramatic thought. My true calling would be as a soap opera actress; I knew it.

My eyes widened. "You don't have to be embarrassed, Robbie. Never apologize for your feelings. It's not like you're stalking or planning to kill Dylan."

"I know." He rubbed his nose, continuing to focus on the new carpeting in my bedroom. "But remember our deal, Cassandra. I'll keep your secret if you keep mine."

The whistling of the wind outside caused me to cock my head towards the window.

***

It was one day several years ago. I was seated on a bench in the park. That was the beauty of living close to a park. I could go there anytime I needed to clear my head because I really fucking I needed it. I was living with a monster, and there was only so long I could trick myself into forgetting about the issue.

I rubbed my eyes while sobbing.

"What's wrong?" called out a voice.

I shifted my focus to the person. "What are you doing here, Robbie?"

He shrugged. "Same reason as you. I wanted to clear my head. Do you mind if I sit down next to you?"

I gesticulated at him. "Sure."

"You didn't answer my question?" His hands fell to his lap. "You don't seem like your usual jolly self."

"I can't help it. I have a lot going on at home."

Robbie's eyes gravitated towards my left wrist. More specifically, my burn mark. "What happened to you?"

I slid the sleeve of my hooded sweatshirt down, attempting to cover the spot. If I covered it, there might have been a chance it didn't exist; I could pretend at least. "It's complicated."

His eyes bulged. "Did your father do that to you?"

"What would make you say that?"

He smirked. "It doesn't take a genius to notice all the dirty looks and eye rolls you give him. But in all seriousness if something is wrong, you would tell me, right?"

"Of course. You would be my first call." I titled

my head back at Robbie. "Now that I spilled my secrets, it's your turn."

Robbie's face drooped. "You have to promise to keep this between the two of us."

Wow. He didn't just ask me that. I could absolutely fucking keep a secret. It was the beauty of being a good liar. "Of course."

"I have a crush on Dylan," he whispered.

* * *

The sound of Robbie's voice brought me back to reality. "Everything okay, Cassandra?"

Okay. I told another lie. I'd concede it. One person knew about my father burning me with a cigarette. But life is filled with dishonesty. The only reason people get mad is because they happened to be pissed off about something else and need a dummy to let their frustrations out on.

"Yeah. I'm fine," I said. "There's something I wanted to ask you."

"And what's that?"

My jaw twitched. "You believe me about the kidnapping story, right?"

"I guess so. But I'm not sure there's much to believe." He scratched the back of his neck.

"What's that supposed to mean?"

He stuffed his hands into his pockets. Wow. The day he gave up basketball shorts was the day he'd be on his deathbed. "I didn't mean anything bad by it. What I said is the truth. I don't really know anything about the last year of your life other than that you were kidnapped."

I wrinkled my nose. "I need to tell you another secret."

His eyes lit up. Robbie's life must have depended on finding out what I would tell him. "Okay. Go ahead."

"I think Lucy has doubts about me being kidnapped."

"That could be possible. It would explain why she's been acting odd."

I didn't know whether it was good or alarming that someone else noticed Lucy's strange behavior. It was good I was letting someone in and being honest (or as honest as I could be). But I also had to think about the other side of the issue. If Robbie noticed something else was up with Lucy, other people would find out too. And it was one thing I couldn't afford because I had to protect my secrets.

"But there is one good thing, Robbie."

"And what's that?" he asked.

"I met a new guy. Chuck something."

"Yeah, I think he's in a couple of my classes." Robbie smirked at me. "He's kind of hot."

"No way!" I chuckled at his comment. "He's mine. You have to back off. Besides, you have your hands full with Dylan."

"Relax, Cassandra. It was a joke." Robbie inhaled a long breath. "I'd never betray you like that. I'm not that cruel."

* * *

I headed into the kitchen hours later after escorting Robbie to the front door.

I scanned the man's body and admired his business attire without even caring about seeming phony despite how caring about appearances was superficial. It was another reality people would have to confront someday, whether they wanted to or not. "Hi, Mr. Brooks! It's good to see your back from your business trip."

"Yeah, I'm glad to be home." Mr. Brooks brought the mug up to his lips while the steam from the coffee pressed up against his face before he blew on it. "How are you adjusting?"

I forced a grin. "Fine, thanks. I really appreciate

how you and Mrs. Brooks have been so generous to me during this difficult time.”

He shook his head. “Don’t worry about it. You’re Elena’s best friend. We couldn’t just leave you to live on the streets or in foster care.”

Mr. Brooks was kinder than most people. He had that going for him, and didn’t have the kill or be killed instinct.

“It must be hard living without a father,” he said.

“Yeah. I guess.” I bit my lip. “But losing my mom before I was one made dealing with cruelty easier. I learned the world isn’t as pretty of a place as people make it out to be.”

Being cynical at my age didn’t matter. It was a universal truth that had to be accepted. The more I knew about the world, the less time I’d spend crying over everything that went wrong. The truth was simple enough even if the implications were damning.

* * *

My high heels scraped the driveway sometime after midnight while I made my way to the curb as specs of moonlight beamed from the night sky. I ducked under a bush once the station wagon became visible. I would’ve recognized the car anywhere—even in the dark.

I opened the door, not even caring about making any noises.

I cocked my head. “Thanks for coming, Paul.”

He nodded. “You’re lucky nobody noticed me. I can’t imagine people would approve. And also, now that I think about it, you should be glad I picked up the call. I didn’t even recognize the number. I can’t believe you found time to get a new cellphone since you arrived back.”

“You know why I called. Besides, have you met me?”

His breathing picked up, forcing me to feel the

weight of each one of his passing breaths. It reeked of beer, and was almost enough to make me throw up dinner. Not that I minded drinking alcohol. I just preferred to drink in style, and have something more glamorous. Like a Margarita. "I can't do it, Cassandra. It wasn't a part of the deal."

"That isn't entirely why I called you. I need to ask you something, and I'd appreciate an honest answer. I promise I won't be mad."

"Wow. That's rich. You're asking me to be honest?"

I gave him a venomous glare. "Cut the attitude. I need to know if you sent me a letter because I got a note saying my kidnapping story is a lie."

I wouldn't hesitate admitting it. Lucy might have looked guilty, but she wasn't the only person who could be responsible for the note since lovers betrayed people all the time.

He scrunched his eyebrows. "No, I didn't. I have nothing to gain from threatening you."

It would've been easier if he blinked, flinched, or looked away. That would've meant I would've been able to blame somebody else besides my sister. But now I didn't have a choice. I would have to confront the truth at some point.

"That's the weird thing." I played with a strand of my hair, twirling it around my finger. "It wasn't even a threat. The person didn't make any demands. I think he or she only wanted to mess with me."

"Do you have any idea who might have sent it?"

"Yes. I do." I looked down at my high heels. Yet another reminder of my beauty and how I was destined for greatness despite the idea sounding like a delusion of grandeur.

"As for the other thing, will at least you think about it?"

He scowled. "I don't know what to tell you."

My sobs mixed with more tears. There was never

a detail that was too small when it came to forcing someone to do what I wanted. "You have to! You don't understand. The detective who interviewed me doubts my story, as do others."

"Do you realize what you're asking me to do? I could go to jail. And we both know I didn't kidnap you. I saved you from your father. Are you really that desperate to protect your 'perfect' life?"

"I'm aware of that. And you should know me better by now. Appearances are everything."

Paul shrieked, moving his hands through the air, hinting at how a person could have guessed he was Italian without any prior knowledge. "You should never have gone out for the soda. You knew the plan. You were supposed to stay hidden."

I sighed. "I got a little careless. I'm sorry."

He pursed his lips. "You're being pretty fucking unreasonable, you know that. I was the one who saved you."

"I know. It's just that plans change."

He shook his head in a vigorous fashion. "I should never have helped you fake your kidnapping."

"You knew what you were getting yourself into."

"I did. So, you don't have to remind me."

"You know I love you." I extended my right arm, squeezing his hand.

Paul gritted his teeth. "You know people are going to be flabbergasted when they find out you're dating a 26-year-old."

Yeah. It didn't matter if I was making a mess out of my life. Still seeing Paul was kind of fun even if I was now interested in Chuck. It was like a plot out of a good soap opera. Although that fact didn't matter. Complications were my specialty. The truth was, living a drama free life was a foreign concept to me after every bad thing I endured. It was kind of fun in a demented way.

I let out a faint laugh. "The age of consent is 16 in

this state."

"That doesn't matter, and you know it."

"I'm begging you. Go to the police station, and confess to my kidnapping. I'm not saying that you'll have to stay in jail forever. I'll come up with a plan."

"I can only promise to think about it." His gaze met mine. "Besides, you know you're scheming will only get you so far."

I pouted. "Please! You know I wouldn't ask if it wasn't important."

"No. I can't agree to it. And if you bring it up one more time, I'll march down to the police station myself and blow the lid off your whole plan."

"You wouldn't do that. You might be homicidal, but you aren't suicidal. That would bring you down too," I said, taking in a long breath. "In case you've forgotten, you're an accessory to my scheme."

"Well I haven't gone to the police and supported you're story yet, so there's no fraud," he said.

"Anyway, is what you said about your father locking you up in the basement for hours true? I mean, I know that I've asked you a 1000 times but I still can't believe it."

"What do you think?"

He glanced down at my scar, which was something my life would always come back to. There was no doubt about it. "I'm glad I wasn't there when your father burned you with his cigarette."

I ran my fingers through my hair, putting it into a ponytail. "Yeah. You're lucky."

"You know, most boyfriends wouldn't help their girlfriend fake their own kidnapping to escape their abusive father."

I didn't even think about my response. "I know. And for that, I owe you everything…"

Fuck. I now had two people to worry about. Paul might not have sent the note, but he was trouble. I could only hope I wouldn't have to make a choice between saving myself and throwing him under the bus. No matter how much bad gossip there was about me being a liar, that was the God's honest truth. God could strike me dead himself if I were lying. It was one thing to be at war with your family but it was another to be in a toxic romantic relationship.

As much as I dreaded making a choice between Paul and myself, the answer was clear. There was nothing complicated about it. I'd choose self-preservation. But just because I had to do it, didn't mean I'd enjoy it.

He frowned. "The next time you call me, it'd better be important."

Yeah. There was a malicious subtext to the tone of his voice. I shouldn't have only been able to call him about something important. He was boyfriend, and I should have been able to tell him anything.

I stepped outside before slamming the front passenger door shut while something howled. It must've been a coyote attacking a deer.

Whatever.

I wasn't the intended prey, so it wasn't my problem.

The ignition made a clunky sound when Paul started the car, and it wasn't long before he barreled down the road. He was soon out of sight, and I was alone like every other moment in my life. Ultimately, I was isolated even when surrounded by people—nobody else could ever know the real me.

# Chapter 4

I ran into Chuck several days later in the school hall-way. I was on my way to first period while other students were huddled together in various spots, en-grossed in conversations with their cliques.

His smiled. "Hi, Cassandra. Good to see you."

I flipped my hair over my shoulders. "Same. I've been thinking about you."

It wasn't all a lie. It was fun to think about Chuck in light of the unpleasantness of Lucy's possible betrayal and Paul's insubordination. It was more than being a dis-traction or needing someone to like me. There was something nice about someone not knowing who I really was, which meant Chuck was my fresh start. He was also kind of nice to look at it.

He tugged at his backpack straps. "Really? Tell me all about it."

I winked. "You. Me. A hot date. It'd be fun."

Chuck remained silent for a second, choosing to have his gaze remained fixated on me. It wasn't long be-fore he laughed. "That's nice. But you ruined things."

My eyebrows inched upward. "How so?"

"I was supposed to be the one to ask you out. Whatever. Maybe I need to learn the value of nonconformity."

I cupped his chin with my hand. It was enough to prick the hairs on my back. "That's gonna be a problem. I never follow the rules."

Chuck didn't move my hand. "I see. Maybe I can make an exception for you."

I yanked my hand away, pulling it to my side. "I also wanted to thank you for something."

"And what's that?"

"I know you're new to town but you must have heard about me on the news by now, not that I'm trying to brag or anything. Although it's just refreshing that you see more than a headline with me."

He took in a long breath. "Don't worry about it. Besides, I've moved around a bunch of times. I know what it feels like to put on a persona."

I couldn't believe it. Chuck shared something personal, so my plan was working. If it could even be called a plan, that was. Sure. It might have been fun to live in the moment. But I was still cold and calculating like my fake kidnapping story proved.

"Would you wanna grab lunch today?" I asked.

He rubbed his Swiss Army watch, which was looped around his right wrist. "I'm sorry, I can't. I'll be in the library during that time—I have a paper I have to write."

"Okay. No problem."

It was the first time somebody ever denied me something. I could only hope it wouldn't become a regular habit since that word wasn't in my vocabulary. People didn't get to where I was by people refusing requests.

He tilted his head, making direct eye contact. "But maybe another time? Who knows, maybe we could have that date someday?"

"Yeah. I'd like that." It was the truth. I had nothing to gain by lying to him. If I wanted attention, I could talk to Paul or cry to Elena and her mom about having flashbacks of the last year. Chuck wasn't expedient yet because he didn't know anything major about my life. That meant I couldn't manipulate him to serve my agenda. Not yet, at least.

* * *

Robbie and Dylan exited the lunch line before Elena and I since we straggled behind with all the choices about what to eat. We decided on salads. It also didn't help that the there was only one cashier working today. As a result, there were at least ten students ahead of us.

"I ran into Chuck this morning," I said, attempting to maintain control of my tray. There was nothing more annoying than being clumsy even if I was only carrying a salad.

Elena moved forward as someone else plowed out of the line. "That's good. Anything new with him?"

"We discussed the possibility of a date."

"That's great. I just hope you're interested in him for the right reasons," Elena said.

"And what's that supposed to mean?"

Another person got out of the lunch line. Although there were still eight kids ahead of us, and the line couldn't move slower if it tried.

"I didn't mean anything bad by it," Elena said.

She must've been figuring out the polite way to say I was a manipulative bitch. Elena still saw right through me even if she was one of my best friends because she always reminded me to do the right thing. I wasn't sure if it was nervy or nice of her. She could have been trying to look out for me since I didn't have a mom. She also could have been a bitch because she had nothing better to do. And that'd be infuriating—Elena wasn't the master of the universe. It wasn't her job to tell people how to behave and to pass judgment on others. That was what adults were for.

We left the line a couple of minutes later.

A guy popped out at me from the corner of my eye. I blinked. It was the same guy I thought it was when I opened my eyes again. It was Chuck.

I narrowed my gaze. "Would you mind waiting a second? I need to talk to Chuck."

Elena nodded. "Of course. Let me know how it goes."

I flocked over to Chuck's table, not even waiting for him to say if I could sit down.

He gasped the moment I sat down. "Oh, hi. I didn't see you there."

I rolled my eyes. "I thought you had a paper you had to work on?"

"I did. I just needed to grab a quick bite first. I wasn't planning on staying for long."

I snorted. "Admit it. You lied to me."

He shook his head. "I never lied to you, Cassandra. I just took advantage of a situation. I really do have a paper to work on, but I didn't feel like socializing during lunch. I used that as an excuse. It's a half-truth."

A half-truth.

The idea was enchanting. The word was the perfect description of my life. Paul was proof of it. I was using him and dating him at the same time because I couldn't risk alienating him after he helped me fake my kidnapping. But I'd have been lying if I said I wanted to end up with him. And that was okay. We weren't meant to last. Paul would figure it out at some point. My mind soon returned to the concept of a half-truth. They were fascinating. It was the perfect way to describe human nature. Nine out of ten times, nothing was ever simple. Appearances weren't just deceiving; they were intoxicating. But if there was one thing I learned in my life, it was even the biggest lie had a hint of truth to it.

"Thank you for being honest." I stabbed a part of the salad with my fork, shoving a bite into my mouth.

"You can go now."

"Sure." I rose after grabbing my tray. "But only on one condition."

"And what's that?" His attention remained on his lunch.

He must've been disillusioned by the idea of a strong girl. It was okay. I would give him time. Chuck would get used to me at some point. He had to if he was going to be my boyfriend.

"I want you to eat lunch at my table," I said.

"Really?"

I sighed. "Yes, really! Why would I invite you to lunch if I didn't want to eat with you? I'm not that cruel."

His shoulders rose. "Sure. But I can't stay for long. I've procrastinated enough as it is on the English paper."

"Of course. No problem."

It wasn't hard to figure out from the way he jumped up from the table that I was probably his first real friend. It had nothing to do with being arrogant. Chuck was just one of those kids. He wasn't bullied. Yet at the same time, he didn't have people lining up to be his friend. It wasn't his fault. People were cast aside all the time. I knew all about it since I'd have to kick Paul to the curb if he continued giving me grief no matter how unpleasant the idea sounded.

If I died right here and now in the cafeteria, I would have been redeemed. A little bit that was. Including someone at lunch was the right thing to do, and was a win-win situation. I would gain and ally and a hot guy to stare at the same time. It would also help me sleep at night knowing the scorching sensation that suffocated me burned a little less. I might have been popular, but I still under-stood how it felt to be swallowed by agony. Certain situations had that intense vibe, weighing the person down regardless of being optimistic.

* * *

There was a knock on my bedroom door while I did my homework that evening.

"Come in," I called out.

The door creaked.

I lifted my gaze off my textbook, tossing it to the side. It wasn't long before I whirled around. "What's up, Lucy?"

She shut the door behind her, slamming it with such force my lamp almost fell off my desk. "We need to talk."

I got up from my chair without pushing it in. I scurried over to Lucy, forcing myself to feel the intensity of her breathing, as if they were anchors about to drag me down to the bottom of the ocean.

"Everything okay?" I asked.

"No. It isn't. I know you're faking your kidnapping story." She put her hands on her hips. "And I also know you met with some guy several nights ago. Let me guess, he's your accomplice?"

That was one thing I didn't miss about being gone: Lucy's attitude. It was one thing to be confidant, but it was another to act like she owned the place. She wasn't a millionaire yet.

I fought the urge to laugh. "Bullshit! You don't have proof."

"I don't need evidence. Do you think it's a coincidence you came back to town within less than a week of Dad dying? Maybe Detective Sanders needs to examine that fact more closely."

I pointed my finger at her. "You want to know what I think? I think you killed our father."

Lucy hissed. Snake was another word to describe Lucy since she always slipped her way into a conversation. "That's ridiculous."

I whipped my head back and forth. "No. It's not. I found the gas canisters and lighter in your bedroom. I guess you should've covered your tracks better."

She ran her fingers through her hair—almost as if she wanted to pull out a clump of it. "You searched my room?"

"Yeah. I did. I was looking for my necklace Elena gave me for my 14th birthday. I know you stole it, and was counting on you saving that from the fire."

Lucy scoffed. "If I were you, I'd get professional help. There's only so long you can continue with your delusions of grandeur."

"What's wrong? Not fun being under a microscope?"

"Don't mock me. Just admit it, Cassandra. You used our father's death to put an end to your fake kidnapping charade."

I almost ripped her head off right then and there since Lucy was anything but sunshine and rainbows. But no. Counting to ten in my head proved best. Couldn't start any trouble. "Fine. I admit it. I faked my own kidnapping to escape our father, and realized his death would help my return," I said.

"Was that so hard to admit?"

It was amazing. It was like everything required more work with her. I could only wonder how much longer the two of us could go on before we both brought each other down.

"I could put pressure on you too, you know!" I didn't take my eyes off her, not even for a moment. Doing so was a luxury I couldn't afford. It'd give Lucy an opportunity to do something twisted.

"Yeah, I killed the bastard. But at least I wasn't a coward."

I gasped. "Why?"

"Do you really have to ask that question? You know what it was like growing up with him."

My heart thumped, getting louder with each passing moment. "Don't ever call me a coward again. Do you understand me? If I recall, I was the one that stepped in when he was going to burn you with a cigarette. Apparently, you forgot to thank me."

The muscles around her lips tightened, as if she ate something acidic. "Okay. You did one good deed. Although doesn't give you the right to act like a hero."

"Let's make a deal." I once again counted to ten under my breath. "I won't get in your way, and you won't get in mine."

"Fine!"

"Because..." I paused for a second since I was never one to miss including a dramatic effect. "If you expose the truth, then I'll drag you down to Hell with me."

There was an eloquent symmetry to the situation even if it was morbid. We were both carrying secrets we would die with, proving we were more alike than either one of us cared to admit.

I'd have a good laugh about the situation later, though. There was no doubt about it. Although I couldn't be sloppy because I was still aware of the issue of hubris even if I had missed sophomore English class.

I couldn't hide from the issue any longer. I was gonna have to be one step ahead of Lucy since my facade counted on it. But if I were being honest, it would have been nice to worry about living my life and not just surviving. Although that'd be tomorrow's problem.

# Chapter 5

Chuck and I went on a date the following Friday night. He suggested going to the movies because that would be a low-pressure type situation, and I agreed with him. There was nothing like formalities to kill the potential of a first date. And I was in a generous mood, so I let him chose the movie. It was some horror movie. I hadn't even rolled my eyes when he suggested seeing that type of movie. Maybe it was because I was twisted myself or maybe it was because I wanted a distraction. I didn't know.

He grabbed my hand halfway through the film, and I didn't even push his hand away. I couldn't blame him for grabbing my hand. The villain in the movie made a frightening reappearance as everyone thought he died in the fire at the beginning of the film. It was also important to feel needed.

He let go once the scene ended.

But the scary scene wasn't the only time our hands touched since our hands brushed up against each other when we both reached inside the popcorn bucket a few minutes later. The hairs on my back stood up. Being with Paul for the last year must have wiped my memory when it came to dating. After all, it wasn't like we had time for romance when we were trying to stay out of the public eye. I bit my lip, realizing I shouldn't have been thinking about Paul while I was on my date with Chuck. It was bad etiquette. I would have flipped out if roles were reversed, and the guy I was out with was thinking about his ex.

Ex.

It seemed like a binary. One could say Paul and I were over. Any feelings between the two of us were fleeting. On the other hand, you couldn't deny we still had a connection. We were in each other's lives despite the lack of trust between the two of us. I didn't have to be a genius to realize he was probably afraid I would throw him under the bus.

There was an old saying my freshman French teacher told me. If you thought someone was watching you, then that meant there was a good chance it was true. I turned my head around towards the end of the movie—almost thinking Paul was in the back of the theatre. I blinked. The person was gone.

Chuck leaned in my right ear. "You okay?" he whispered.

I nodded, attempting to push the matter out of my mind. I could wait till the following day to think about what I would do about my fake kidnapping story/whole Paul situation since it wasn't unreasonable to want one night to pretend to be a normal teenage girl.

It was still a joke. If I were being honest with myself, then I'd have to admit I forgot the meaning of normal a long time ago.

***

Chuck was nice and walked me all the way from Elena's driveway to the front door a couple of hours later.

I grinned. "Thanks for a good time."

"No problem. I was happy to take you out. We should do this again sometime."

I swallowed the uneasy feeling in my throat. "That'd be nice."

A silence ensued between the two of us for a couple of minutes. Wow. I never once considered how I might have a "normal" problem, because I would've killed to deal with mundane, awkward situations when I was at my father's mercy.

He hesitated. "So…"

I didn't even so much as blink. "I know you wanna kiss me."

"I don't know what you're talking about it." His cheeks became flushed in a matter of seconds.

"You don't have to be ashamed." I pulled him without giving the matter another thought.

We were caught in the embrace for a good couple of minutes before we pulled back from each other.

I hadn't even mattered if I had been too flirtatious—I did what needed to be done. Besides, being with Chuck was the opposite of mixing oil and water. Almost as if we were opposite sides of the same coin—opposite, yet still complemented each other.

He licked his lips. "That was something, Cassandra. Maybe we should do that again."

"Maybe next time."

"You're saying there's going to be a next time?" he asked.

A gust of wind swooshed through the air, causing my hair to bounce around in twenty different directions, which meant fall was coming. Whether it was invited or not. "Yeah. I think so. We'll talk soon."

* * *

I ran into the kitchen sometime later—a few minutes before bed—only to clap my hand over my chest when I saw who was standing there in front of me. "Oh, Lucy, you've gotta learn not to be sneaky."

She crossed her arms. "What are you doing up?"

"I needed to find my charger." I reached in one of the kitchen drawers, searching for my charger. It took a good minute for me to find it. Elena's mom really needed to go through the all the papers. I mean, how many recipes did this woman need?

Lucy winked. "How's Chuck?"

I turned around to face her. "How do you know about Chuck?"

She lunged forward. "I saw you guys kissing through the window."

"You were spying on us?" The idea was unbeliev-able. I might not have been perfect, but at least I knew where to draw the line. It appeared that was a lesson Lucy still needed to learn, though. I guess as with all things, it took time. The sooner the better, as far as I was concerned. I couldn't have her spying on me all the time. She was al-ready suspicious of me as it was.

"Don't be so melodramatic." Lucy brought her mug up to her lips.

No wonder why she was so on edge. There was no reason for her to be drinking coffee so late into the even-ing.

"What's a matter? Afraid I found real happiness?" I demanded.

Lucy snickered. "I'm not terribly worried. You'll ruin things with Chuck all on your own. It's what your good at."

I sighed. "It doesn't have to be like this Lucy? I don't expect us to be best friends but it would be nice if there was something between us besides disdain."

"You ruined that chance a long time ago. Or have you forgotten?"

"Are you still mad about the whole kidnapping

thing?" I asked.

She placed the mug on the counter, sliding it to the side. "It's not even that."

Lucy remained silent for the longest time, then grunted. "Does the first week of November a couple of years ago ring a bell?"

The trees bobbed in the wind, making the roaring sound smack up against the entire house.

* * *

I was back at my previous house with my suitcase right next to me when I heard footsteps moving around Lucy's bedroom.

I walked into the foot of her bedroom, giving my sister a look. "Everything okay?"

"Yeah. I'm fine," Lucy said, not even bothering to look me in the eye as she kept tossing things into her suitcase.

"Are you going somewhere, or something?"

She spun around before making her way a few feet in my direction. "When are you going to get it, Cassandra? I have to get out of here. I can't take it another minute."

* * *

The sound of Lucy's voice brought me back to reality…

"Do you remember that week or not?" she demanded.

"I was going to Maryland with the debate team that week." I brought my arm up to my mouth, expelling a quick cough.

If she were a teapot steam would have oozed out of her head at the moment. "That's not all. If you recall I was planning to leave town for good. But then our bastard of a father found out and locked me in the basement until you got back."

I clapped my hand over my mouth with my free hand. There was nothing dramatic or phony about my reaction. Whether I wanted to admit it or not, there were still some things that terrified me.

She screamed. "You told him I was gonna escape, didn't you?"

Just because we didn't get along, didn't Lucy should've assumed the worst in him. We were still sisters, and I'd never hurt her for real. Even if the same couldn't be said for her attitude towards me.

"I did no such thing. You have to believe me," I stammered.

"Liar!" Lucy drew in several deep breaths. "Ratting me out is something you'd do."

"I didn't do it. I swear it."

"No offense or anything, but your word doesn't mean shit."

"Do you really hate me so much that you're willing to punish me for something I didn't do?" I asked.

Lucy didn't say anything, yet she didn't have to. I knew the answer before I even asked the question. It was disheartening to think somebody could be capable of such vindictive thoughts. She was worse than me. I didn't entirely blame her. It must have been awful being stuck in the basement for a week. I only hoped our father had the decency to feed her.

"How do I know you aren't lying?" I asked, refusing to look away from Lucy.

"You just don't get it, Cassandra! You can't make up something that's this fucked up."

She had a point. I might have had a twisted imagination, but even I knew the truth was stranger than fiction at times.

Lucy smirked. "Tell me something, Cassandra? Do you even care about Chuck, or are you using him so you can throw him under the bus to take the fall for something?"

Okay. I would give her points for one thing. She wasn't that far off. Lucy just had the wrong fall guy.

"I would never do that," I said. I forced a gulp of

air into my lungs, realizing what I had to do. Eye contact was the only way I would sell my next point. "Anyway, you have to believe that I'm sorry for what happened to you."

Lucy gritted her teeth. "I don't have to do anything. As far as I'm concerned, you might as well be dead. You should have just done us all a favor, and stayed gone. But I guess that would have been too easy."

***

I returned from my jog the following morning to find Mrs. Brooks and Detective Sanders on the front porch. Then, my heart fluttered while my mind raced with numerous thoughts. I so wanted to deal with the detective.

I put my hands on my hips. "What are you doing here?"

Detective Sanders forced a grin. "Hello, Cassandra. I was just telling Elena's mother that we can't put off the questioning any longer."

"Am I under arrest?" The blood burned through my veins faster while it shot in all directions throughout my body.

"Not exactly," said Detective Sanders. "But it'd be helpful to go over the facts of the case, because we still really don't know anything about your last year."

I elevated an eyebrow. "Are you accusing me of lying?"

She drew in a breath. "No. But I'd be lying if I didn't say things looked a little suspicious. However, I'll give you props for one thing. You know how to put on a good act. I mean, you've only returned one of my phone calls, and have blown off the others even though I impressed upon you the urgency of our meeting."

Mrs. Brooks pushed her sleeves up. "Are you really blaming the victim? She has been through hell you know. It's natural she'd be a little shaken up when it comes to the details. Also, haven't you taken into account the fact she was probably blindfolded a lot. But you know what else I think? The real issue isn't her story."

Laughter fell from Detective Sanders's mouth. "It isn't? I don't suppose you want tell me how to do my job now, do you?"

Elena's mom shot the lady a dirty look. "The fact remains, you questioned a minor without an adult present."

"She wasn't a suspect." Detective Sanders tugged at the sides of her blazer, getting rid of the dust.

Whatever. It was nice I had one adult in my life. Even if it was my best friend's mom.

I was wrong about one thing—Paul and Lucy weren't my only problems. Detective Sanders was becoming a pain in my ass, because she was smart enough to realize I was blowing off our follow up interview. So, I couldn't play dumb no matter how stupidity seemed like the easiest defense.

* * *

I opened the front passenger seat door sometime after midnight. "Thank you for coming, Paul."

Paul scoffed. "It wasn't like I had a choice. You were hysterical on the phone."

"I stalled the detective for now, but the only way she'll believe me is if you come forward and say you kidnapped me."

"And why would I do that?" he asked.

I shifted my gaze, deciding to look out the window even though the air was drenched in black. "Because it was tearing you up and you wanted to do the right thing."

"I said it before and I'll say it again. I'm not going down for a crime I didn't commit. You might be hot, but you aren't that hot."

"If you don't tell the Detective you kidnapped me then I'll tell the police what you were doing in Mexico during the third week of June."

Mexico.

It was the one week Paul left me by himself. I would never be so grateful to get involved with a man who had a shady background as I was in this moment.

His jaw lowered. "You wouldn't."

My nostrils flared. "I would. If you drag me down, then I'm bringing you right to Hell with me."

Paul sucked in a breath. "Fine. I'll do it."

I couldn't believe it. This was really gonna happen. I manipulated someone into confessing to a crime that he didn't commit. It was actually kind of scary when I thought about it. Paul was wrapped around my finger, and there wasn't a damn thing he could do about it. He was there to serve me no matter what.

So, I'd just have to hope Paul wouldn't betray me. He couldn't. Even Paul wasn't that dumb.

# Chapter 6

Robbie and I went to the mall several days later, and were currently at a store on the second floor. We were still looking at the various clothes and outfits.

He held up a dress. "What about this? You would like nice in it, don't you think?"

I resisted the urge to laugh. Robbie had been kind enough to waste part of his afternoon even though he told me he had a test the following day. "I'm not so sure about that," I said.

Robbie exhaled a breath, not even saying a word.

I didn't have to read his mind to understand what was bothering him. It was a safe guess. Dylan. The only issue was whether or not I should bring up the problem. On the one hand, it could mean I cared about him and was trying to take an interest in his life. On the other hand, it could be seen as intrusive. I'd feel that way if a person caught me in a bad mood and I was in Robbie's shoes.

But we were best friends, which meant we were supposed to tell each other everything. If I couldn't tell my best friend something then you couldn't tell anyone the thing.

I lifted my gaze off the table, focusing on Robbie instead. "Do you wanna talk about it?"

"I don't know. There's nothing to really talk about." His eyes remained on the dresses while he continued to glance around at the selections on the table.

"You shouldn't be ashamed for how you feel. I've seen the way Dylan looks at you with his intense eye contact and body posture. It isn't all in your head. I mean what guy notices when another guy bleaches his hair blonde?"

His face drooped even more. Robbie might as well have burst into a fit of tears right here and no. "It's just so hard, Cassandra. I feel like I'm damned either way. If I tell him, then he'll never speak to me again. And if I don't tell him I'll be consumed by the whole situation until my death."

I picked up a dress from one of the tables, then surveyed it. "But you could tell him and get everything you want?"

"Yeah." Robbie forced a laugh. "If by get everything I want, you mean humiliation."

"Don't be so hard on yourself." I put the dress under my arms. I was gonna have to try this one on. The evocative nature of the sapphire color was something I couldn't run away from. Besides, everyone knew I'd love a good show.

Robbie rubbed the side of his neck.

"Do you want me to say something to Dylan? I'd be happy to? Sometimes, it's easier to have a friend tell someone something?" I asked.

He glared at me for a moment. "I don't know. That might not be a good idea."

I wasn't offering to tell Dylan the truth to put Robbie on the spot. I thought it'd genuinely help him. I might not have been in the exact same position Robbie was in, but that didn't mean I didn't know what it was like to be consumed by secrets. And if there was anything I learned, there were two ways to handle a secret. A person could let the secret consume them alive like a fire or take control of it. It was obvious which option was better. I couldn't imagine anyone that would want to be chained down by something.

* * *

I returned home to Elena's house after Robbie dropped me off to find Mrs. Brooks waiting for me on the living room couch.

I shuffled over to her, putting the bags down on the table before opening my mouth. "Is everything okay?"

"No. Detective Sanders wants you to come down to the police station and make an ID. Someone walked into the police station and confessed to kidnapping you."

I smacked my hand over my mouth. "Damn. I can't believe it."

She sighed. "Anyway, we should get going. I told Detective Sanders that we'd be down at the station as soon as you got home from school."

"You believe me, right?" I patted my gold bracelet on my wrist. "I'm not lying."

"What I think doesn't matter," Mrs. Brooks said. "Anyway, let's go. We can talk about everything later."

I didn't know whether I should be happy or mad. Mrs. Brooks could have been hinting at the fact she knew I was lying or she could have actually meant there was no time to talk about something that was a baseless accusation. It didn't even matter if I was lying. Detective Sanders was supposed to give me the benefit of the doubt. I wasn't some sociopath. I was just a teenager to the rest of the world. There was no way a teenager could pull off such a big lie even if it would be funny to see Detective Sanders's head pop off when she found out the whole thing was a sham.

* * *

I was seated in a conference room at the police station an hour later.

Detective Sanders pushed the photograph in my direction. "Is that the person that kidnapped you?"

Mrs. Brooks looked into my eyes. "You know that there isn't a rush right, Cassandra? You can take as long as you want to identify the guy."

"But not too long," Detective Sanders said. "We have to decide if we're gonna hold him or release him."

Mrs. Brooks shook at her head at Detective Sanders's comment.

I took the photo, being sure to examine it. I couldn't respond too quickly. It would be a dead giveaway that something was up. "Uh…Yeah. That's the guy. I'm sure of it."

* * *

I walked towards the holding cell at the police station the next morning, smiling at how the universe was on my side for once in my life.

Paul's transfer to the general prison hadn't occurred yet. Although people might eventually wonder how I even knew that if I ever got caught. Well, here was the truth. I could hack my way into anything, including blacking out the security cameras at the police station for the next twenty minutes. It also helped that I was dressed as a police officer and it was the changing of the shifts, which meant there was a little lag time before the police station would be crowded.

Paul's eyes widened. "What are you doing here, Cassandra?"

"I might be a bitch, but I always keep my word." I

grabbed the keys from my pocket, making a clinking sound once the key turned in the lock. Then, I offered my hand. "Come on. Let's leave."

"How are we just gonna walk out of the police station?" he asked.

"Don't worry. I have it all figured out. There's a hallway we can take that leads to a back exit facing a street that's usually deserted at this time in the morning. I have a car. It'll be fine."

We made our way through the hallway. Sweat dripped down my face when the scurrying of footsteps echoed right as I reached for the door.

Paul and I stepped foot on the sidewalk, then headed towards the car. I got in the driver's seat, and he got in the front passenger seat.

"I thought you didn't have your license." He put his seatbelt on.

I put the key in the ignition, letting the car warm up. "I don't. But I have my permit. Don't worry, I'm a good driver."

"Where are we going?"

I stepped on the gas, plowing down the road and out of sight. "I'm gonna take you to the bus station. I have a bag in the backseat, which has money, sunglasses, a new fake I.D. and social security card, a wig, and a bus ticket."

He gasped. "Wow. You thought of everything. But in all seriousness, how did you get the car? And where are you sending me?"

I couldn't believe Paul was still unaware of how I operated after all this time. Planning getaways and fake kidnapping stories was the kind of demented things I thought about all the time. I had quite the life, really.

"Florida." I hit the brakes right as the light turned red.

Paul let out a nervous laugh. "I guess I should be glad you're sending me some place warm."

There was nothing menacing about his voice. It

was plain like when I first met him. Helping me fake my kidnapping story must have taken a toll on him. There was no denying it. Being reminded of what drew me to Paul in the first place was nice in a nostalgic kind of way.

I parked the car by the curb half an hour later. Paul and I were standing in line at the bus stop.

A screeching sound rolled up the street. The bus was here.

"Goodbye." Paul leaned in, then kissed me, yet I didn't pull back.

The embrace lasted for a good minute before Paul headed up the line and onto the bus.

The bus barreled away in the opposite direction, leaving me by myself.

The wind picked up, pushing a few leaves and crushed cans down the street. Yet another sign fall was coming, which meant winter would arrive before I wanted it to.

"What are you doing here, Cassandra?" called out a voice.

I turned around. "I could ask you the same question, Chuck."

He crossed his arms. "You first. And why are you dressed like a cop? And why were you kissing some guy?

Shit

Just when it seemed the universe was on my side, things had to be fucked up. And I couldn't deny the truth—I was gonna have to concoct a big lie to get out of this debacle.

# Chapter 7

"Fine." I counted to ten under my breath. "I'll tell you everything, but not here."

He nodded. "Okay. Let's go to my car."

I followed him back to his car, allowing him to guide the way.

"What the hell are you up to?" Chuck asked once we were seated in this vehicle.

I bit my nail. "I faked my kidnapping story."

"Are you for real?" Chuck demanded.

No offense to Chuck, but he shouldn't have acted surprise. Doing so wasted my time. Besides, his reaction proved he might not have known me as well as I hoped. Or maybe I was just impatient and expected the entire world to revolve around me. Yeah. That could've been it. Or maybe I was being too hard on myself. All my abuse from my father might've made me wanting people to go along with my every whim—including understanding my theatrical qualities.

"Yes," I said. "But there was a good reason. My

father physically abused Lucy and me as kids, and I couldn't take it anymore."

Chuck didn't say anything. But no surprise there. Some reactions couldn't be presented in beautiful sentences.

"But then I used his death as an excuse to come home in addition to how my boyfriend was starting to turn on me," I said.

"Have you been seeing this guy all a long?"

I shook my head in a vigorous fashion. "Not entirely. I haven't slept with him since before I came back to town. I swear it."

"Why did you kiss him?"

I took in another gulp of air. Breathing was my only option at the moment—whether I liked it or not. "I only did that to save face."

"Oh," Chuck said. "What about us? Do you actually like me, or are you using us as an excuse to run away from life?"

"Do you really want an honest answer?"

"Yeah, I do." Chuck didn't take his eyes of me.

I tilted my head towards the window, choosing to look at the people that flocked down the street instead. "It was a little bit of both."

He took out a tissue from his pocket, then wiped his eyes. "At least you're being honest."

"Are you crying?"

"No. It's just allergies." He shoved the cloth back into his pocket.

I patted his shoulder. "You don't have to be embarrassed. I'll be the first person to admit I've cried more times than I'd like to."

He pushed my hand off his back. "No, I'm fine. Anyway, are you gonna leave the other car here?"

"Yes, I think I will. That way the car can't be traced back to me."

"I'll drive us back to town."

I almost choked on a gulp of air. "You aren't gonna tell anyone, are you?"

"Relax. Your secret is safe with me. As for us, that might be a different story."

I sighed. "It doesn't have to be like that if you don't want it to be."

He raised his hand at me. "Save it! You don't have to play me to keep me silent. I never break my promises, so you can move on to the next guy."

I did it. I was 100 percent honest with someone. I had never done that before. There was just something damning about opening myself up to another person. I hadn't even been completely honest with Paul. It was to be expected, though. Victims of physical abuse couldn't allow themselves to be vulnerable. They had to protect themselves even after their abuser was gone. The world was a cruel place. No amount of spinning the situation would make life better.

* * *

Dylan and I hung out at Starbucks the following day after school, and we were at a table in back.

He planted his lips onto the whipped cream, then ate a bite of it. "Why did you want to hang out? Don't get me wrong. I'm happy to hang, it's just it isn't really are thing. No offense, or anything."

I furrowed my eyebrows. "What are you talking about? We're friends."

"Forget it," he said. "What's up?"

My elbows slid up the table. "I see the way you mess with Robbie"

Some of his Frappuccino dripped out of his nose. "What are you talking about?"

"Save it, Dylan. Everyone can notice your intense stares, body posture and occasional weird comments."

"What are you saying?"

"It's wrong. Either you see Robbie as more than a friend. Or you can be his tolerant, straight best friend. You can't have it both ways, though." I reached for my cup, bringing it up to my lips. There was nothing the explosion of the sweetness of the caramel and the bitterness of the espresso that was the Caramel Macchiato. And it was just what I needed. Both tastes balanced each other out. It was as simple as that.

"Are you saying that Robbie likes me?" Dylan asked.

"Yes. And it's tearing him apart."

Dylan sighed. "Thanks for bringing it to my attention. I'll have to handle him."

"Be sensitive about it," I said.

"Are you really telling me how to handle letting down my best friend?" He grabbed his Frappuccino, not even thinking twice about gulping down a third of it.

* * *

I was at my locker the next morning at school when someone tapped my back. I whipped my body around. It was Robbie.

He started sobbing. "What the hell is wrong with you?"

I snickered. "What are you talking about?"

"Dylan talked to me about my crush." He jabbed his fists through the air. "And that means one thing. You told him the truth."

Fuck. Maybe I should've waited for Robbie's official confirmation before helping him with his problem, because rage would've pulse through my body if roles were reversed.

"It didn't go well?" I asked.

He screamed even louder this time, making his voice echo through the hallway. "You think? I can't believe you, Cassandra! You're supposed to be my friend.

Are you that bored with your life that you have to mess with other people?"

A burning sensation formed in my stomach. "No. I was just trying to help you."

He undid the top button of his blazer. Wow. His fashion tastes bordered on pretentious. I mean, who the hell wore a blazer to school?

"Since you dropped a harsh truth, I'm going to drop one as well," he said. "Nobody believes your kidnapping story, which means it's only a matter of time before you drown in your lies. Also, nobody likes you. You're just as bad as Lucy, maybe worse. You're nothing but a spoiled, stupid, selfish brat. And the only reason why Dylan, Elena, and I are friends with you is because we'd rather have a forced friendship than an enemy."

Robbie clipped down the hallway without another word.

"Well, well, well, it looks like you're having quite the morning," said someone.

No need for the lady to state the obvious.

I rolled my eyes. "What are you doing here, Detective Sanders?"

"I want to talk to you about Paul Weston." She folded her arms. Wow. Detective Sanders must have been preparing for battle or something. "He disappeared from police custody the other day. There's also a brief black out on the security footage."

"What are you saying?" My heart pounded, becoming louder with each beat.

"Either there is a mole on the inside, or someone hacked and snuck into the police station to break him out. My money is the latter."

"You can't talk to me without Elena's mom. I'm a minor."

She scratched the back of her neck. "You aren't under arrest. This is just a friendly chat."

I cackled, hoping I'd prick the hairs on her back.

That bitch needed to know I wasn't a person to mess with. "Maybe if the police would do their jobs, then there wouldn't be runaway criminals."

"You want to know what I think?" She paused. Apparently, I wasn't the only one who stopped at certain times to create a dramatic effect. "I don't think Paul was ever a criminal. I think you and him hatched up the fake kidnapping story together. I just can't come up with the motive."

I laughed at her again, not even caring about disrespecting her. She was a bogus cop, after all. "Wow. You should write a novel. At least then people would buy the bullshit you're selling."

"I wanted to give you an opportunity to be honest. If you are in some kind of trouble, then now's the time to speak up."

"I could have Elena's mom sue you for harassment."

"I guess we'll be doing it the hard way." She started walking away in the opposite direction before turning back at me. "I look forward to seeing you again sometime under less pleasant circumstances."

Detective Sanders was out of sight in the blink of an eye.

Back to Robbie. I wasn't trying to be mean by outing Robbie's secret to Dylan. I was actually trying to help him. Even if nobody believed me. Robbie wasn't a game to me. He was my friend. I would never intentionally do something so cruel. I had nothing to gain by it. If I wanted to have a toxic banter with someone, I would talk to Lucy. Whether I liked it or not, I was going to have to come up with a way to fix everything. I couldn't let Robbie hate me. Our friendship was supposed to last forever. There was no debate about it.

* * *

The doorbell rang hours later in the evening when I was in the kitchen, making a cup of tea since I couldn't sleep. I made my way to the front, almost shaking my head when I saw who stood on the front porch.

"What are you doing here, Chuck? If you came to yell at me, I'm really not in the mood."

"I didn't come here to yell at you. I came here to have you that is if you still want to be with me."

My eyes lit up. Christmas was coming early this year. "Yeah, I do."

Chuck pulled me in for a kiss, placing his hands on my cheeks. We remained caught up in the embrace for a good five minutes, choosing to tune out the rest of the world. Or least that was what I did. It was my only option. Everything else was tomorrow's problem.

I wouldn't even worry about if it seemed like I was using Chuck because nobody else wanted to deal with me at the moment. That'd also be tomorrow's problem. Besides, now that Paul was gone, I needed a new partner in crime. And it wasn't like Lucy or Robbie volunteered.

# Chapter 8

I grabbed Chuck's hand, guiding him back to my bedroom while we ascended the staircase. There was something refreshing about doing something so simple. Maybe it was because of all the lies I told since my return home. But whatever it was, it didn't matter. The only thing that mattered was being in the moment, which meant Chuck deserved all of my attention.

I made sure to shut my bedroom door before pulling Chuck in for an embrace. He wrapped his hands around my cheeks. I inhaled his cologne, taking in the mixture of earthly and sweet scents. I extended my hands, reaching for his shirt. It wasn't long before I lifted the shirt off his body, tossing it to the floor. Like it didn't matter.

We got onto the bed after a few more seconds went by. His mouth pressed up against my neck while I ran my fingers through his hair, noticing it was smooth. Wow. He must have used a good conditioner, and I would have to get the name of it after we hooked up. What was I thinking? I should have been more concerned about being in the moment with Chuck.

He pulled his head away from my neck, making sure to look me in the eye. He didn't have to say what he was gonna ask me. The question was written all over his smile. I nodded at him. We shed all of our clothes without giving it another thought. He moved up and down, sounding vibrations across the bed while he pressed against me. I didn't even have to think about Paul to get off, which was nice. There was only so long a girl could handle being with the same guy.

He got off me sometime later, deciding to be on his back. "That was something."

I rubbed sweat off my face. "Yes. It was."

"Was that your first time?" he asked.

"Nope. What about you?"

Looking away didn't matter. His face turned bright red. "Yeah, you were my first. I hope you won't hold that against me."

I nudged his shoulder. "You worry too much. Has anyone every told you that?"

"Everyone I know. So, what's one more person?"

Giving it up quickly didn't matter. It felt right in the moment. There was something about Chuck, which was different than Paul. It hit me after thinking about it for another couple of minutes. Chuck wasn't judgmental like Paul. I told him the complete truth and was rewarded whereas with Paul, he might have helped me, but he still gave me grief every step of the way. It was nauseating when I considered the entire situation. Paul was no angel even if he would never admit what he was doing in Mexico that week in June. I still knew the truth because it didn't take a genius to put two and two together.

He licked his lips. "What are you thinking about babe?"

Babe.

I didn't know how I was supposed to feel about him using that word. It was more affectionate than anything Paul did. I was lucky if Paul ever kissed me outside of the bedroom.

My eyebrows knitted together. "There's something I wanted to ask you if that's okay with you?"

He nodded. "You can ask me anything."

"Why don't you judge me like other people do?" I needed to look him in the eye when I asked the question. It was probably because of the paranoia from all of the times my father lied to me.

Chuck took in a deep breath. "It's because people have judged me over the years, and I hated it."

"Interesting. Anyway, thank you for the honest answer. There's something else I was wondering if that's okay?"

He quirked an eyebrow. "And what would that be?"

I looked away from him. This whole honesty thing just wasn't meant to last. "I did something really bad, and I don't know what to do."

Chuck extended his arm, cupping my chin. "Are you okay?"

"You know of Robbie and Dylan, right? I've been best friends with them for years."

He nodded again.

"I told Dylan, Robbie has a thing for him, but it didn't go well. And now Robbie isn't talking to me. But I didn't do it to hurt him. I genuinely thought he wanted me to do that. I had nothing to game from being mean," I continued. "Do you think I'm a terrible person?"

"No. I don't," Chuck said. "My advice would be to let the situation work itself out. Sometimes doing nothing is the best thing a person can do. I should know."

I would give him points for one thing. His idea was novel. I hadn't heard it before. Perhaps that was why I gravitated towards him. He offered a new perspective that nobody else could give me. It was more than him being a new. He just possessed a practical attitude. He must have lived in some big city before moving here. I was sure of it.

It was the only explanation that made sense.

* * *

Elena and I hung out the following day in the library during our free period.

She took her focus off her textbook, turning her attention to me. "Do you wanna talk about the whole Robbie and Dylan situation? Promise I won't judge."

I fidgeted around in my chair. There was just something uncomfortable about the library. It was a safe bet that I was allergic to the library. It was like oil and vinegar. The library and I weren't a good combination.

"You probably think I'm a terrible person," I said.

"I don't presume to know anything. But I have to ask you this as your best friend, were you trying to hurt Robbie?"

I shook my head. "How can you even ask that question? I'm not that evil."

She twirled a strand of her hair. "I didn't mean it like that."

"I slept with Chuck last night," I blurted. Wow. I would have to learn self-control. I only imagined what would happen if I told a secret to the wrong person. The result would be detrimental.

"You did what?"

I flipped to the next page of my textbook—I could pretend to focus on my Chemistry homework. "It just happened. I told him some stuff and he ended up being more understanding than I thought he would be."

She scribbled something in her notebook. "That's good."

"You aren't going to continue to judge me?" I asked.

Elena remained silent for a minute. "No. Not this time. As long Chuck makes you happy, then I'm happy for you."

"Thanks. I appreciate it."

It appeared Chuck and Elena had something in common. It was nice. Maybe there was hope for Robbie if Elena learned not to judge me. My shoulders tensed. I couldn't bullshit my way out of this situation. There was only one person to blame for the current mess I was in. Me. I was the one who went to Dylan behind Robbie's back. It seemed like a good idea in the moment even if everything didn't work out. It wasn't farfetched though. Friends helped each other all the time. I still hoped I'd find a way to make things write. I wasn't going to let Robbie become another teenage suicide statistic. Not on my watch. Plenty of bad things happened as it was.

* * *

Dylan asked me to meet him in the park that day after school. I didn't even have to think about my answer. There was a lot I needed to discuss with him.

I sat on the bench while tapping my feet on the ground. Dylan texted saying he stuck in traffic and was going to be a few minutes late. I couldn't get mad at him. He tried to do the nice thing.

The rays of sunlight pushed through the cloudy sky. Wow. Perhaps summer wasn't dead yet.

"Sorry I'm late." Dylan sat on the bench.

"Don't worry about it. Anyway, mind if I talk first? There are some things on my mind."

"No problem."

I coughed. "I want you to know how sorry I am about the whole situation. You have to know I never meant to hurt you or Robbie."

Dylan sighed. It was the only thing he could do. "I know. You don't owe any explanations. It's not like I hate you."

I looked down at the ground. "Well, you should. Everything has gotten fucked up."

"The truth is, I've known Robbie has liked me for a long time. I just didn't want to say anything."

My eyes widened. Dylan wasn't gonna get out of this one so easily. "Then why do you play with him?" I asked.

He shrugged. "I don't know. I guess it's kind of nice knowing somebody likes you."

"It's not a nice thing to do, Dylan. Robbie is your friend. He deserves better unless there's something more I don't know, so by all means tell me…"

"I sent Robbie an email when I let him down."

"You did what?"

"I know it's kind of impersonal, but I that was the best thing to do. I was really trying to look out for him. I didn't want him to be more humiliated than he already was." He put his hands behind his head, locking his fingers together.

"You shouldn't have done that. Robbie probably thinks you're afraid to be around him."

He pouted. "But that's the thing, Cassandra. I'm not afraid to be around him."

Shit. I just couldn't believe it. Even I was smarter than Dylan. Sending someone a rejection over email wasn't the thing to do. It was even crueler. I couldn't blame Dylan 100 percent, though. It was understandable to be concerned about how somebody would react in person. I'd be lying if I said I was never concerned about how Paul reacted to certain things I told him. It was nerve-racking to say the least.

I almost bit my tongue while I thought about the matter more. "If it makes you feel better, Robbie hates me."

"It doesn't," he said. "But thanks for trying."

A silence ensued for a couple of moments.

I forced a grin. "Give it time. I'm sure your situation will improve."

"There's something I have to tell you, Cassandra.

Rejecting Robbie had nothing to do with reciprocating."

Okay. Perhaps the situation was about to get juicer despite how I shouldn't have treated my friend like some sort of entertainment.

I frowned. "What are you saying?"

"I feel the same way about Robbie that he does about me. I like him as more than a friend."

# Chapter 9

Dylan and I stood in my bedroom a couple of hours later. I stared at the floor while he paced back and forth. The door creaked not too long after that.

"What's the big emergency, Cassandra? This better be important. I was in the middle of a *Gossip Girl* marathon," said someone

I smiled at him. "It is, Robbie. Relax. I love *Gossip Girl* too, and I wouldn't pull you away from that if it wasn't necessary."

Robbie rolled his eyes. "What's he doing here?"

"He has to tell you something," I revealed.

Robbie crossed his arms. "I don't need to be rejected again. Once was enough."

I glared at Robbie. "Just shut up and listen! You might actually be glad you came. Trust me."

Robbie's nostrils flared. "Doubtful. But go ahead. Give it your best shot."

I turned to Dylan. "Go ahead. I think it's time."

"I lied to you, Robbie. Your feelings aren't one sided," Dylan said.

"I don't understand what you're getting at," Robbie said.

Dylan put his hands in the pockets of his leather jacket. "I like you like you."

"But you said you didn't feel the same way about me," Robbie said.

"I was lying." Dylan paused for a moment. "That's why I've kind of been playing with you. It isn't all in your head."

Robbie scoffed. "What do you mean kind of? You have been playing with me. You know it. I know it. Cassandra knows. And I'm pretty sure the rest of the world knows it."

Dylan coughed, clearing the scratchiness in his voice. "And you're right. It was wrong of me, and I have no excuses. I hope you can forgive me."

Robbie glanced at Dylan, then me, before settling on Dylan. "How do I know this isn't some twisted joke?"

It was a fair question. I would've asked the same thing if I were him.

I counted to ten under my breath, remembering that Robbie was in a fragile state at the moment. "It isn't. Not this time. I have nothing to gain. I'm just doing this to help two people I care about."

Robbie put his hands on his hips. "Even if that were true, that doesn't change the fact that we're only in this mess because of you."

"I know. And I truly am sorry. You have to believe me," Dylan forced out.

"I don't have to do anything. I'm so over this bull-shit. I'm out of here." Robbie left my room in a matter of seconds, then the door slammed shut.

The echo ringed in my ears for a moment before I summoned the courage to speak. "I'm sorry, Dylan. I know this wasn't what you expected."

"Damn right. I thought you said things would go fine?"

I shrugged. "I don't know. Robbie must be in a mood or something. It's the only logical explanation."

"You're gonna make this right. Do you understand me? Because as harsh as Robbie might have been, he was still right about one thing. This situation is all your fault, and it's time you owned up to it. We aren't dolls you can use for your own enjoyment."

* * *

I beat Elena and Lucy down the stairs the next morning, yet I almost screamed in shock when I saw Mrs. Brooks. The events of the previous evening must have been tugging at me more than I realized. If the situation weren't so tragic, I'd laugh at it. Robbie got what he wanted, only to toss it aside. It wasn't like Robbie. He was the last person I'd expect to be childish. Robbie must have been more confused than he let on. It was understandable. One minute Dylan said he just wanted to be friends and then the next minute he said he wanted to be more than that. It was enough to blow anyone's mind.

"Everything okay?" Mrs. Brooks asked.

I walked over to the cabinet, then pulled out a mug before tilting my head back in her direction. "Yeah. I just have a lot on my mind. I'm sure it will be okay, though"

She finished the rest of her coffee, then put the cup in the sink before opening her mouth. Mrs. Brooks must have too preoccupied to care about putting the mug in the dishwasher. "There's something I wanted to talk to you about."

"Did I do something wrong?"

She exhaled a breath. "I would like to think of myself as an open-minded person, but the next time you have a friend sleep over please have the person give their parents a credible lie. Chuck's mom called me and gave me hell."

"Sorry. Didn't mean for that to happen."

"It's fine. Just don't let it happen again."

I swallowed the bit of coffee in my mouth. I hadn't even bothered to put milk or cream in it. It was that kind of morning. I needed strong black coffee at the thought of trying to get through another day.

"I won't. Don't worry," I said.

She smiled, revealing her well-aligned teeth. "Good, I'm glad. Although don't get me wrong. I'm glad you've made a new friend."

"Thanks," I said. "Chuck seems to be a great guy."

She tugged at the sides of her jacket, straightening it. Elena's mom must have been more neurotic than I thought. "Yeah. He's a great guy. He's a little quiet, and might come across as odd, but that isn't his fault. He's a good kid."

"How do you know him?"

Mrs. Brooks shook her head. "He moved to town shortly after you were kidnapped."

At least Mrs. Brooks was still under the impression I was kidnapped. Either that or she wanted to save face. I couldn't tell which scenario it was, not that it mattered or anything. I didn't have to give the matter a second thought. She was an ally against Detective Sanders. It was all that mattered.

Wait.

She just said Chuck moved to town shortly after I was kidnapped, meaning he has been here a whole year before I came back.

Wow. I wasn't the only one who knew how to tell a good lie.

"Are you sure he's been in town for a year?" I asked.

"Yeah. Why?"

"He said he just moved to town this year. Whatever! I must have misheard him."

She blew a loose strand of hair out of her way. "Yeah. That must be what it was. He's a good kid. I don't think he would lie to you."

* * *

Chuck walked up to my locker half an hour later at school. He pulled me in for a kiss, and I didn't even hesitate. It wasn't till we pulled back from our embrace that I remembered my conversation with Mrs. Brooks.

I crossed my arms. "I know you lied, Chuck. What's going on? I know you're hiding something."

"What are you talking about? You aren't making any sense."

I almost spat at him right then and there. "Cut the bullshit. I know you've been in town for the last year. I want to know why you lied."

"I thought it would make for a more interesting story if you thought I was new to town. But I'm sorry I lied to you. I never meant to upset you. You have to believe me."

I shoved the last book I needed into my backpack before zipping it up a moment later. "It's fine. Just don't let it happen again."

Okay. Chuck was more dangerous than he appeared, and I'd have to take note of that.

"It won't," he said. "You have my word."

"Anyway, there was something on my mind. Elena's parents are going to be out of town this weekend, and are leaving us without adult supervision since her mom prides herself in being progressive. And I thought it would be a good opportunity to throw a party. It's be fun. You could get to know my friends. What do you say?" I shut my locker door, making sure not to slam it.

"I don't know about that."

I nudged him in the shoulder in a playful fashion. "Come on. What's a matter? Do you have skeletons in your closet, and are afraid you're going to run into someone you're trying to avoid?"

His face turned white in a matter of seconds. Wow. It wasn't his day.

"It was a joke," I said. "Anyway, it's okay. We don't have to throw the party. I just thought it would be fun."

Chuck glared at me. "Don't do that. I'm not some dumb little puppet. I know you're trying to manipulate me, Cassandra."

"I'm not; I swear. It really doesn't matter to me either way."

"Fine. Let's do it. I'm game."

* * *

I strutted into the kitchen hours later after returning home from school. My fifth cup of coffee for the day was the only way I was gonna get through my homework. Unfortunately for me, someone else was there. Lucy.

"How's the evil bitch today?" Lucy asked.

"You know something, Lucy? You're so broken that you don't know how to lead a normal life."

She snickered. "That's rich."

"It's true. But it doesn't have to be this way, Lucy. Our past doesn't have to define our present. You can start over."

She inched forward. My sister was so close the whatever mouthwash she just used prickled my skin. "I heard about your party. "

I recoiled since I could only begin to speculate what Lucy would do to me. "Congrats, Lucy! You found out I was throwing a party without Elena's parents knowing. It wasn't like I was going to exclude you."

"It wasn't like you had a choice. I live in this house." She took the cap off, then brought the water bottle up to her lips. She gulped down the water for a good ten seconds before placing the bottle on the counter. "Relax. I'm not going to rat you out."

"And why is that?" I asked.

Her smile widened—almost as if she was the Cheshire Cat. "It'll be another opportunity for you and Chuck to self-destruct. I overheard your little fight in the hallway, and can infer it's only a matter of time before he throws your lying ass to the curb."

Lucy shouldn't have been like this. I might not have been perfect. I could concede that. But I wouldn't concede having a sister that was always consumed by the darkness. It was unhealthy. I also meant what I said. Lucy didn't have to behave like a bitch. This was her opportunity for something different. Even if she wouldn't admit it.

"You still can't be mad about that other thing? You weren't the only one who was affected by the basement. I didn't want to say anything but the evening you hung out at James's house, he locked me in my bedroom without supper and wouldn't let me out till the following morning." I hesitated for a moment before going on with the rest of the story. "That's why I burned you with his cigarette. But no offense, you aren't that innocent. He made you push me down the stairs if I recall. So, I guess that makes us even."

Her hands fell to her sides. "I'm not talking about that, and you know it."

* * *

I walked with Elena in the school hallway the next day to first period.

"I'm going to throw a party at your house this weekend while your parents are out of town, and I was wondering if you could help me plan it," I said.

"And were you even gonna ask me for permission?"

I tugged at my backpack straps instead of looking

Elena in the eye.

"Relax." She giggled. "I was giving you a hard time. I'm down with a party."

"Okay. Good." My chest crashed up and down a few times. "But don't worry. I'm not a complete brat. I know I'm a guest in your house, so I'll clean up after the party."

Elena snickered, causing her voice to become louder this time. "Please? You clean up? I'd pay to see that happen."

I didn't know why, but for the rest of the day something Chuck said bothered me. I just couldn't get over the fact he lied to me. It wasn't only my wild imagination. He had to be hiding something. I was sure of it. Either that, or he had been embarrassed, and was just trying to impress me. Both situations were possible. But it didn't matter. I was gonna get to the bottom of things. Hell, I'd even go as far and say I'd bet my life on it.

# Chapter 10

I ran into two guys holding hands on the way to lunch, and I grinned even if the sight was unexpected. It was nice something went well for once.

"What's going on here?" I asked. "The last time we all talked, this seemed like the last thing that would happen."

Dylan pulled his hand away, then sneezed into his sleeve. "We talked between then and now."

"It turns out we didn't have as many issues as we thought we did," Robbie interrupted.

I clapped. "You have no idea how exciting this is. My party is gonna be so hip this weekend now that the school's hottest couple will be there."

Dylan rolled his eyes. "You're throwing a party? When did that happen?"

I waved my hand through the air. "That part isn't important."

"You do know we aren't doing this for attention, right?" Robbie's teeth poked his lip.

I forced a gulp of air into my body. "Yes. I know

that. Can't you guys take a joke?"

"You're right." Robbie sighed. "I can be a little uptight sometimes."

"More than a little." I chuckled. "But that's okay. That's why you have Dylan to help you."

Dylan smirked. "What did you just say?"

"Okay. Maybe that comment was out of line." The grin remained on my face. Robbie and Dylan's reconciliation was proof anything was possible. And I'd just have to hope that Paul's possible reappearance wasn't one of those things. It was the last thing I needed.

A silence ensued for a couple of minutes. I'd have to come up with more ways to say, "I'm happy for you guys" during my free time.

I glanced at the both of them. "Can I ask you guys a question?"

They nodded at me, which was another example of how that would be one of many things they would be doing together.

"How did you put up with Lucy while I was away?"

Robbie coughed into his arm. "You mean when you were fake kidnapped?"

It was an important question even if Robbie decided to be annoying. If I had been in the gang's shoes, I wouldn't have been able to put up with Lucy.

"That question is easy," Dylan said. "She's your sister. We didn't have a choice."

The lump lingered in my throat. "Yeah. That makes sense. Thanks for doing that. You have no idea how much of a difference you made in her life."

"It was that bad?" Robbie reached for his water bottle, then chugged it down in a matter of seconds.

"You have no idea." It was the truth. Lucy needed to know she wasn't alone despite what she might have felt when she had to endure our father all by herself.

It was something to think about at night when I

couldn't fall asleep. Lucy could have come with me. There was no reason why she had to endure the abuse alone. Although it would have seemed slightly suspicious if we both disappeared since our father would have known something was up. It was something I would live with for the rest of my life. There was no debating it. But there was one thing I didn't have any doubt about. I'd find a way to rationalize the situation. It was what I did best—my worst enemies couldn't even deny it. Not even Lucy.

"I just want you guys to know if anyone gives you a hard time, they'll have to answer to me," I said. The offer was genuine. I had nothing to gain by standing up for them.

Robbie snorted. "I don't think that's gonna be a problem. Things aren't what they use to be."

Yeah. That was true. Everything changed. It wasn't even all for the better because there were a lot of things I had to think about even if I didn't want to. The fact that my sister and I were both keeping secrets was one thing. I never imagined I'd fake my own kidnapping and that Lucy would be responsible for killing our father, which brought up another issue. I would keep Lucy's secret. The man had it coming. I wasn't gonna shed a tear over a man I couldn't even call my father. Not now. Not ever.

Footsteps squeaked against the floor. The three of us tilted our heads. It was Lucy. She clipped down the hallway without even smiling at us. Whatever. If she was in a bad mood, that was her business. I wasn't going to let her ruin my day. I already had enough bad days to last a lifetime, not that it would stop the universe from reeking hell on me.

* * *

Someone tapped my back while I stopped at my locker after lunch.

I spun around, almost shrieking when I realized it was Lucy. It was probably the black eye shadow that pushed her appearance too far. There was no reason for her to be walking around like she was. There was no denying it. She was beautiful, which meant she didn't need something like eye shadow to make her appearance pop. It didn't even matter if I was being hypocritical since I loved makeup and accessories as much as the next girl. There was something fun about dressing up. I could pull it off. Lucy couldn't. The answer was easy. She was a simple person. I wasn't. Anyone would see through her façade in a matter of seconds.

I furrowed an eyebrow. "What do you want?"

"I wanted to apologize." She paused, suggesting she needed my approval to continue, which was kind of odd. Lucy never sought my permission.

"Yeah. Sure. Give it your best shot." I shoved the books into my backpack, zipping it up a moment later.

"We've been getting off the wrong foot, and it shouldn't be like that. We're sisters. We're all we've got."

My heart stopped beating for a minute. This couldn't be the real Lucy. Somebody must have swapped places with her. The real Lucy would never say something so nice. I had a better chance of getting an alcoholic to stop drinking.

"I'm not trying to look a gift horse in the mouth, but why now?" I demanded. "You could have done this at any time. How do I know you aren't trying to manipulate me?"

She sneered. "Do you really think I'd be so obvious about it if I was trying to manipulate you?"

It was a good question. There wasn't an easy answer. It was still way too early to engage in psychological warfare at this point in the day. My head already had Chemistry to thank for that.

"I don't believe you. You don't have one good bone in your body." A scorching sensation burned on my left eyebrow, forcing me to rub the spot.

"There are things you don't know, Cassandra."

I lunged forward. I couldn't let Lucy get away with trying to intimidate me. "I doubt that. Anyway, even if what you are saying is true, there's still no reason for me to trust you."

"I kept your fake kidnapping story a secret," Lucy said. "That has to count for something."

I cackled at her without even blinking. "But don't forget I know you set the fire, dear. So, it's a two-way street."

Lucy ran her fingers through her hair, examining it. And if she were a friend, then I'd tell her which conditioner she should have been using.

"Look, Cassandra, can you please shut up?" Lucy asked. "There's something you need to know."

"I'm not interested." I shut my locker door before darting away in the opposite direction.

Hubris.

It was another word that could describe me. Knowing what I know now, I should have finished my conversation with Lucy. Whatever. I would just chalk up my arrogance to another foolish young mistake. Nothing bad could happen to me. I was Cassandra Jenkins. I was invincible. The rest of the world were the people that had bad things happen to them.

* * *

My party arrived in no time. It was the event everybody was going to be talking about. The party was so big that conversations were going on in every room of the house while alcohol continued to flow into people's red cups. People could thank my fake I.D. for that. As far as the people at Fair Lake Spirits were concerned, I was 21. It was yet another thing to be proud of. There wasn't anything I couldn't get past people. The music was also a nice touch to the party. It was loud enough to be considered "blasting," but just quiet enough for the neighbors not to call the cops.

Chuck and I greeted people at the door since he came over early to help me set up.

The door opened. It was Robbie and Dylan. They were even holding hands.

I winked at them. "You two look nice. Don't they, Chuck?"

Chuck nodded. "Yeah. They do. It's good to see you guys."

"Same," Robbie said.

I gesticulated at the two of them to stop hovering in the door and to actually come into the house. "Can I get you two guys a drink? We have rum, tequila, vodka, gin, whiskey, wine, beer, sprite, diet soda, and probably a few things I don't remember buying."

"I think we can make our drinks." Dylan took Robbie's hand, guiding him through the masses of people and into the living room.

* * *

I had to go to my room halfway during the party to charge my iPhone. Not that I could complain or anything. The battery had lasted me a good 24 hours, which was more than I could say for my previous iPhone.

I almost dropped dead when I entered my bedroom. There was a man—or who I assumed to be man since the person appeared to be tall—sporting a gas mask. I clenched my neck with my spare hand. The man inched closer to the entrance, and my back hairs rose.

The man lunged forward, grabbing my neck before I could do anything. This couldn't be it. I couldn't have my obituary say I died at a rager. That would have been really tacky. The grip around my neck tightened, leaving me gasping. I did the only thing I could think of. I jerked my leg up, hitting the guy in the crotch. After that, I gave the guy a good shove, smacking my head into his head.

I might have defended myself, but I wasn't going to stick around to see who was behind the mask all by myself. I needed help…

I ran downstairs, and found Chuck in the kitchen. "I need you to come upstairs to my bedroom. There's an intruder."

"Yeah, sure," he said. It was good he didn't even ask any questions. Yet another way he wasn't like Paul.

We ascended the staircase, arriving at my bedroom a couple of minutes later.

Chuck scanned the room before cocking his head back at me. "There's nobody here, Cassandra."

It was true. I moved around, gazing at my bedroom myself. This couldn't be.

"I don't understand," I stammered. "You have to believe me, Chuck. There was a man in a gas mask standing here only a couple of minutes ago, and he tried to choke me. I'm not lying. I swear it."

He squeezed my hand. "It's okay. I believe you. You don't have anything to prove to me."

I didn't care what Chuck thought. There was a man in a gas mask. I would have bet my life on it. The real issue wasn't the why as opposed to the person behind the mask. I saw Lucy downstairs while I was on my way upstairs, which meant it couldn't have been her. And Robbie, Elena, and Dylan were talking to some of the other guests. So even if Robbie and Dylan hated me for messing with their relationship, it couldn't have been them. I was also sure it wasn't Paul. He knew what I would do if he returned to town without my permission, which begged the question of who the hell it could have been.

The weirdest part was the person had been standing there, meaning he was waiting for me. And that meant I must have known the person.

Yeah. There was no doubt about it.

I wouldn't sleep till I found out the truth. Somebody tried to kill me—whether I wanted to admit it or not.

# Chapter 11

I shuffled over to my locker the following Monday morning to find another surprise. The gas mask wasn't the only thing I didn't want to have to deal with.

I put my hands on my hips. "What are you doing here, Detective Sanders? You can't tell me you actually enjoy being a scab that won't die."

She quirked an eyebrow. "I have proof that you weren't kidnapped."

My heart thumped, getting louder with each passing beat. "What are you talking about?"

"Somebody sent us security footage from a hotel in Miami, showing you. You want to know who else it showed? Your friend, Paul, which backs my theory you were never being held against your will."

I almost spat at her right then and there. It didn't matter if she was a cop. There was nothing to respect about her. The bitch wouldn't quit till I was behind bars.

"Are you arresting me?" I put my hands in my pockets.

Her head moved back and forth, becoming faster

with each moment that went by. "No. Not yet. I want to build an airtight case against you before I bring anything to the District Attorney."

I flipped my hair over my shoulders. "This constitutes harassment, Detective Sanders. You can't appear at school to talk to me because regardless of what you think of me, I don't show up at your place of business to give you a hard time."

"I think the situations are a little different, don't you?" she asked.

My sneakers squeaked across the ground after I moved towards her. "Not really. But I do have one question. Why do you hate me so much?"

She pulled her blazer together. "I was just like you when I was your age."

"What changed?"

She snickered. "I grew up."

I stomped my feet. And most people must've thought I was crazy, because I was wearing sneakers instead of heels. But no. I wasn't crazy. Fashion was another thing that changed as much as my mood swings. I then kicked my feet again. The detective had to know who was in charge. There was no debate to be had about the matter.

"You know what I think, Detective Bitch?" I asked. "I'm gonna tell Elena's mom you talked to me by yourself, and then we'll see who is laughing."

Detective Sanders stared me down, refusing to let me look away. This method must have been how she broke criminals. "I was actually doing you a favor. I doubt you want Elena's mom to know you're a big, fat liar."

A burning sensation formed in my stomach. I was gonna have to get a water bottle from the cafeteria before first period. I really should have been drinking more fluids. Being dehydrated wouldn't help me.

"It would be nice if the police would actually do their job in this town," I said.

Her eyebrows inched up. "And what's that supposed to mean?"

"Somebody broke into my house this past weekend, and tried to choke me." I took my hand to my eye, rubbing it.

She held in a breath for the longest time before it blew out of her. "I highly doubt that. But even if you were telling the truth, why didn't you report it?"

My jaw trembled. "The man was gone when I came back with help."

"Forgive me if I think you're exaggerating."

* * *

I was silent while I walked to class with Chuck later in the day. I didn't even bother holding his hand. There were too many things to think about. I would decimate Detective Sanders if it was the last thing I did. The bitch didn't know when to give up. She must have been jealous of me. I already accomplished more than she had even though I was only 17. It made sense. I would have been bitter if I were her. I didn't know what I would do if my ass got fat because of too many donuts. I would tell her to lay off them the next time I ran into her. I only hoped it would be enough to make her cry. I wanted her to feel the emptiness I felt every time she talked to me. Fair was fair.

Chuck feigned a smile. "Is everything okay, Cassandra? I don't mean to pry, but you seem quiet today. Did something happen?"

I turned my head, almost fainting when the blood vanished from my face. "Do you want the truth, or do you want me to make up a lie?"

He frowned. "The truth. I think you owe me at least that, don't you?"

I sighed at him. He had a point. "Detective Sanders talked me this morning, and says she has security footage from a hotel, which proves I was never kidnapped."

"Is it true? I promise I won't judge you. I just want a real answer."

Bullshit. Chuck would absolutely judge me. Humans always judged each other. It was something that couldn't be avoided. Like an unwritten law of physics.

I started to sob a little. "Yeah, it's true. I went on a vacation with Paul in Miami for a week."

"You did what?"

We turned the corner, trekking down a new hallway.

"It's true," I said. "I was mad Paul went to Mexico so I told him I wanted to take a trip."

"Wow." Chuck fumed at the comment. "You keep putting my family in a positive light. I don't know whether to thank you or scold you."

"Don't be melodramatic. It isn't an attractive color on you."

His Adam's apple throbbed. "Okay. Good to know."

"I just wish I knew who tried to break into my bedroom the other night at the party. Because no offense or anything but I don't care what you think. I know what I saw. I could have died."

"Did you tell Detective Sanders about it?

I came to an abrupt halt. "Don't be ridiculous. That bitch wouldn't know how to find her way out of a grocery store."

The worst part about being targeted was not knowing who was after me. That meant I wouldn't be able to vanquish my enemy. It didn't even matter if the idea was obvious. It was true. You couldn't win an invisible war. Luckily for Detective Sanders, the person in my bedroom was a lot taller her. If it wouldn't have been for that, I would've skewered her alive.

* * *

I knocked on Lucy's bedroom door hours later in the evening. There was no telling if she tracked down the security footage and sent it to Detective Sanders even if she couldn't be the person who donned a gas mask in my bedroom.

"Come in," called out a Lucy.

I pushed my way into the bedroom, not even caring about the door slamming behind him. Then, I placed my hands on my hips. "We need to talk, bitch!" I exclaimed.

She lifted her gaze off her textbook. "What did I do now?"

"Did you send something to the police department?"

"No. I didn't."

A bead of sweat rolled down my face. "Give me one good reason why I should believe you?"

She stood, not even bothering to push her chair in. "You know I started the fire, so you could bring me down. I therefore have to keep your secret."

"I don't know about that, Lucy. You're certainly meaner than you let on. I wouldn't be surprised if you stole social security checks on the weekends."

"That's rich, Cassandra. I might have killed our father, but I'm pretty sure that you killed our mother."

"Are you kidding me? We have never met our mother. She died before we were one. So how could you even say something like that?"

Lucy needed serious help. If she believed what she just said than she suffered even more from delusions of grandeur than I did. And that was say something.

I scoffed. I was also guilty of delusions of grandeur if I thought I was going to get away with everything without coming up with a bigger lie. Lies were my safety net. They were the only constant in my life. They never disappointed. I must have been there during that day in kindergarten when they told us lying was bad. It wouldn't have made a difference. I was who I was, and nothing would change that. I shouldn't ever have had to bow down to other people. The rest of the world were the ones who should have been kneeling at my feet. I shook my head. Even I didn't always know where my digressions were going. I didn't have time for it. I would keep focused on one thing, and one thing only. Getting Detective Sanders off my back. It was all that mattered. She caused me enough grief as it was even if she was an incompetent detective. I would have to pray she got run over by a car or something. Okay. Maybe getting run over by a car was a little harsh. She didn't have to die. A cruise to Antarctica would suffice. I would buy a fake cruise for her, signing the note as an anonymous secret admire. The thought was laughable. As if somebody would ever like her. That was like saying the Devil did good things.

* * *

I tossed around in my bed that evening. The image of the gas mask person remained burned in my mind. Knowing who the person was, wasn't just necessary for satisfying my curiosity. I needed the truth in order to sleep at night.

* * *

I woke up a few hours later, grabbing the iPhone that was on the table beside my bed.

"Give me a call. We need to talk. I think it might be time for you to come back to town, Paul. Anyway, please call me as soon as you get this. If you don't, then I'll burry you." I pressed END before tossing the iPhone back on the table.

I shouldn't have been sweating the situation as much as I did, because if I played things right, I'd be able to to end my gas mask problem and Detective Scab issue in no time. It'd be my masterpiece. It was a promise.

# Chapter 12

I approached Robbie and Dylan in the school hallway before first period a couple of weeks later.

"I was thinking we should go out on a double date," I said, refusing to take my eyes off the two of them, because if I stared at them long enough, they would have no choice but to agree.

Dylan winked at me. "Really? What made you think that?"

I pushed a chunk of my hair behind my left ear. "I don't know. I just think it'd be nice for Chuck to feel included in the group."

"Are you sure you don't have an ulterior agenda?" Robbie asked.

I sighed. "Yeah. I'm sure. I don't have another motive. Can't we all be friends?"

Robbie looked at Dylan, then back at me. "Yeah, I guess."

"Great. Sounds like a plan," I said. "I'll text you guys later in the day with the details."

Dylan scoffed. "You really don't want us to lie for

you, and help sell your fake kidnapping story?"

"How do you know the story is fake?" I asked, starting to stutter a little bit. There was only so long I could go on without acting nervous. It was a natural reaction. The truth would come out whether I liked it or not. The only question would be how I would spin the situation to my advantage.

"Just a hunch," Robbie said. "We've known you long enough."

I tugged at my backpack strap. "All joking aside, is everyone treating you fairly? I'd hate for someone to be giving you a hard time."

Dylan snapped his fingers at me. "Leave it alone, Cassandra. The school has bigger problems than Robbie and I dating."

I grunted. "Excuse me for looking out for my friends. Can't you guys see I'm trying to turn over a new leaf? I'm not the same person I use to be. That has to count for something?"

"Yeah, we can see," Robbie said.

I didn't even bother to ask what he meant by it. That wouldn't' help me. I only had one thing on my mind these days: destroying Detective Sanders. I didn't have a choice. She made it her life's work to take me down and I wasn't about to let somebody do that to me. I deserved better. Whether she wanted to admit it or not, she was going to have look elsewhere if she wanted to be responsible for the arrest that caused the trial of the century.

* * *

I caught up with Chuck several hours later on my way lunch. The two of us even held hands. It was actually kind of sweet when I thought about it. Paul never wanted to hold hands with me. But Chuck wasn't Paul. I already knew that even if I wasn't 100 percent ready to admit it.

I shifted my focus towards him, making the grin on

my face widen. "I was thinking we should go out on a double date with Robbie and Dylan."

Chuck shot me a brief gaze. "Really? What makes you say that?"

I pulled my hand away from Chuck. "Why? Do you have a problem with them dating? If you do, then I don't know if you and I should be dating."

"It's not that. I'm not sure if it's the right time. There's just so much going on. Especially with that bitchy detective hovering behind you every step of the way."

I hissed at him. Wow. I couldn't have sounded more like a snake if I tried. "You did not just say that."

"You know I'm not trying to upset you, Cassandra. Robbie and Dylan are great guys, and I'm genuinely happy for them. And I don't have a problem with their relationship." He paused for a second. "But if this is something you want to do, then you'll know I'll support you no matter what."

We continued walking down the hallway.

Having a double date wasn't a part of my agenda. If I wanted the three of them to lie for me, I would have said so already. But I didn't. At least not yet. Double dates were supposed to be a regular facet of high school, and as such, I would milk it for everything it was worth. I wasn't about to let another day go by without trying to pretend to be a normal teenager. If there was one thing I learned from my own fake kidnapping story and the fire, it was that you had to take advantage of opportunities while you could. It didn't matter if regret was some overused mantra. It was real. I of all people should have known it. After all, it would have been nice if things were different between Lucy and I. But no! It was meant to be. We would be forced allies at best.

* * *

Elena and I went swimming in her pool after school. Yeah.

I forgot to mention Elena's house has an outdoor pool. Although the two of us didn't make it ten minutes in the pool since we were feeling kind of cold. It didn't matter if it was still technically summer for a couple of more days. Fall was already here. And winter would be here before no time.

I stretched my arms and legs on the chair, hoping to soak up some of the fleeting rays of sunlight.

Elena moved around in her chair for second, attempting to get comfortable. "What's new with you? I feel like we haven't talked in ages."

"Robbie and Dylan are going out on a double date with Chuck and me."

"That's great. I'm sure it'll be a lot of fun." She propped herself up, forcing herself to sit up straight. "There are all great guys. I'm sure they'll get along."

A bee buzzed, causing my eyes to focus in on it right away. "There's still one thing that bugs me."

"And what's that?" Elena reached for her beverage that was on the table next to her chair, yet a small part of me wondered if it was spiked with booze. That would've been the fun thing to do.

I snapped my neck, allowing my hair to fall behind my shoulders. "I want to know what Chuck is hiding."

"You still don't know why he lied to you?"

I rolled my eyes. "He claims he was just trying to brag. But the thing is I'm not so sure if I believe him. Did you guys ever notice him during the year I was gone?"

"No not really." She shrugged. "But then again we travel in different social circles. I'm sure I haven't met over half of the Junior class."

"Yeah. I suppose that's true."

There was no way Chuck meant me harm. It was impossible. I had been alone with him on numerous occasions, giving him ample opportunity to hurt me. It must have been some sort of silly misunderstanding. I was certain of it. He wasn't like my father and Paul. He wasn't going to leave me wounded and confused. Those sentiments were things every girl told herself when she started dating a mysterious guy. There was one difference with me. I meant it. Bad things didn't happen to me. I was Cassandra Fucking Jenkins. I ruled the world. Nothing could go wrong. There were only minor setbacks in my universe. And they were easily fixed. My life was supposed to be perfect. It was the law of nature. Anything less than perfect was unacceptable. There was no debate about it.

The wind whistled, sending chills up my back. I had no choice but to wrap the towel around me. Tanning would have to wait till another day. Besides, I could go to the tanning salon if I really wanted to add some color to my skin. It wasn't a big deal. Girls like me did that all the time. It was a rite of passage about being a teenage girl, at least for the girls in our town.

She chugged the rest of her drink. "Is there anything else you wanna discuss?"

My insides burned. There were still some things that scared me even though I was invincible all the time. "I don't care what everyone else thinks. I still think someone tried to kill me the night of the party."

"Did you ever see the man in the gas mask again?" Elena asked.

I swallowed the uneasy feeling in my throat. "No. But I'm not lying. You believe me, right?"

"It doesn't matter what I think, Cassandra. The rest of the world has already judged you."

"There are things you guys don't know."

She leaned in a little closer. Her life must have depended on my answer, not that I thought she thought I was that important. I wasn't that dumb. "Like what?" she asked.

"Not today—I'm just not ready. But don't worry. I really will tell you the complete truth someday."

"I hope so," she mumbled.

I was being honest. I thought about the issue a million times. There was no way around it. I was gonna have to tell my friends the truth at some point. It wouldn't be as terrible as I thought it would be, though. It didn't even matter if Lucy agreed with me or not. This was something my friends had to know. My father abused me over and over again. It was something I could snap away. The pain was real to the point it was palpable. There was no way of dancing myself out of that situation. At least not yet, anyway. I had to add the not yet part. I was always finding a way to slither out of situations. It was my specialty.

I closed my eyes, attempting to tune out the rest of the world. There was no way I was gonna succeed with my master plan if I was sleep deprived—I needed my wits about me to play these twisted chest games.

The pitter-patter of rain splashed onto the ground, getting louder with each drop. I woke up. Elena was gone. Well, that was rude of her. She could have woken me up before she went back inside unless maybe it was still sunny when she went indoors.

"I missed you," called out a voice.

I tilted my head, gazing to the left of the butterfly bush. "What are you doing here?"

The intensity of the red hue on his cheeks increased with each second that went by. "You're the one who wanted me to come back. Don't you remember?"

"That was two weeks ago." I resisted the urge to yell at him. "Why didn't you return my phone calls?"

He chuckled. "What can I say? I've been busy."

"If this has anything to do with those Mexican drug lords, I don't want anything to do with that."

"Fine. Have it your way." He made his way over to the chair Elena sat in earlier. He certainly had a lot of guts. I couldn't believe him.

We both stared at each other for a couple of minutes.

"What exactly do you need help with?" he demanded.

I stuttered. "Everything. No offense or anything, Paul, but we might have to revisit that whole you breaking out of jail thing."

He shook his head at me, uttering profanity under his breath.

Too bad for him. We were gonna discuss all the options. Even if it meant throwing him under a bus to save myself. I didn't have a choice. Playing dirty was fair game now. He wasn't a little kid—he was 26. If he was stupid enough to get played by a 17-year-old, then so be it. I wouldn't waste any sleep over it.

# Chapter 13

I left Starbucks on Main Street the subsequent afternoon while a woman approached me. Great. It was Detective Sanders. She was the last person I needed to deal with. I was still unsure how I was gonna get out of the fake kidnapping situation. It would require a lot of thought. But I would find a way to solve my problems. I had to. I wasn't ready for game over. I always landed on my feet regardless of the situation. This time would be no different. Besides, I was smarter than Detective Sanders. I knew how to play the game. She didn't.

She feigned a polite expression. "Good afternoon, Cassandra. I see you took your Caramel Macchiato to go?"

"How do you know I like Caramel Macchiatos?" I fought the urge to sweat. Showing panic wasn't an option. I had to be calm and couldn't let the bitch know she was rattling me.

"I didn't."

My eyebrows arched. "It was a trick question?"

"Yes, it was. I figured you are probably calorie

conscious but would order something a little more sophisticated than a plain cup of coffee but something that had less calories than a Frappuccino."

The wind roared, pushing litter down the sidewalk.

"Either that, or your stalking me. Anyway, just tell me what you want because you've wasted enough of time as it is," I said, not even hesitating to give her a dirty look. She wouldn't win. Not this time.

She clicked her lips together. "We know your partner in crime is back in town."

I twirled a strand of my hair. "What's your point?"

Detective Sanders sighed. "I wanted to give you one last opportunity to tell the truth. You don't strike me as evil even if you're full of shit. Maybe this started as a prank or someone is forcing you to do something you don't wanna do."

"Those are a lot of a big assumptions to make."

"I can tell you aren't going to be of much help. But you know where I am if you change your mind."

Detective Sanders walked away in the opposite direction. Wow. I couldn't believe the nerve she had. It was ridiculous. Detective Sanders needed to be knocked off her high horse ASAP. I couldn't kill her. I wasn't about to kill her just to cover up one big lie. I'd give her one thing. She was persistent. But she was even stupider than I first thought since she had no qualms about talking to me without a parent, which in this case was Elena's mom. She said it herself, though. I wasn't under arrest. Not yet. It was just a friendly chat. It was bullshit as far as I was concerned. I would take her down for making my life a nightmare. I didn't care about doing the right thing. She needed to pay for being a nuisance.

* * *

I called Paul later in the day from my bedroom about arranging a meeting on an old side road a few blocks away from Elena's house. I couldn't take a chance of Lucy finding out about another clandestine meeting. I had enough problems as it was, and I wasn't about to add another to the list.

***

A mosquito buzzed around my face sometime after midnight, then I squashed the bug without flinching.

I arrived at his car a few minutes later, then tilted my head when I sat in the front passenger seat. "We have a big problem, Paul."

He snarled. "Yeah, we do. No offense or anything, Cassandra, but I'm getting tired of meeting late at night. I'm not your little bitch, so you can't just order me around whenever you want."

My pulse drummed in my ears while I struggled to speak. There was something different about dealing with Paul than Detective Sanders or any other female. As much as I wanted to be a strong girl, I couldn't. Not entirely. There must've been something unnerving about how a man had the potential to throw me around like some psychopathic child who beat up his toys time after time without any regard.

I clench my jaw. "Look. There's a new plan. I want you to go back to Detective Sanders and tell her you blackmailed me into forcing you escape. You can say you a friend on the outside deliver me the message."

"How would I even get a friend to do that? I was in police custody?" Paul asked.

"It's simple. You were just being questioned. You were never actually arrested, which means you still had your cellphone with you and could have thus easily contact anyone."

He huffed. "But why would I turn myself in again after escaping? It just isn't any sense. I guess you never paid attention in school when they taught you about logical."

"It's simple. Just tell her I'm forcing your hand since if you won't go to the police, I will." I wouldn't know how I managed to say that with a straight face. But it didn't matter. I just had to the idea out there. It wasn't my job to sell the story to Detective Sanders.

He grabbed my left arm, pulling harder with every passing second. "Do you realize how ridiculous this sounds, Cassandra? The reality is, that you're using me as a means to an end. We both know it. So, don't waste your breath denying it. The only reason we are in this trouble in the first place was because you got bored playing house, and wanted to come home."

That wasn't entirely true. My father's death had been the perfect excuse to return back to town since Paul was becoming a problem even back then.

"Let go of my arm! You're hurting me." I tried to push his arm off mine even though the attempt proved futile.

Paul's grip tightened even more. It was now becoming clear to me. I hadn't handled Paul as much as I thought I had.

* * *

Robbie, Dylan, Chuck, and I had our double date the following evening, agreeing to go out for sushi since that was rather informal.

Robbie cocked his head at me after the waitress finished taking our orders. "Are you okay, Cassandra?"

"Why would you ask that?" I reached for my soda, then took a more than generous sip.

Robbie shrugged. "If you don't want to talk about how you got your black eye, then that's fine."

Chuck shot me a look, forcing me to roll my eyes and return my attention to the illustrations of geishas that donned our placemat.

The front door of the restaurant opened, and my mind drifted back towards the rest of my conversation with Paul yesterday.

* * *

Paul released my arm after few more seconds. I didn't wait around for him to say anything else. I pushed the car door open. Unfortunately for me, Paul was fast, and caught up to me within a matter of seconds.

"Where do you think you're going, bitch?" He grabbed my arms, throwing me against the side of the car, which made me bang my head. I'd have to chastise him for giving me a black eye later. Being pinned down was the only thing that mattered.

I didn't say anything. I couldn't. No lie would convince him he was making a mistake.

He leaned up against my ear, and my stomach twisted in ten different direction, "You aren't gonna get out of this so easily. If you think I'm going to waste any more time covering for your cheap ass, then you have another thing coming. Here's the new plan. You're going to finance the rest of my exile."

"How much do you want?" I asked.

"10 million dollars."

My mouth gaped. This was such bullshit! The tables couldn't turn on me. I was Cassandra Fucking Jenkins. Nobody ever put me in a corner. "I don't have access to that much money," I said.

His breathing prickled my skin. There was nothing comforting from this warmth since the hairs on my back pricked up. "Well, you better," he said. "If you don't get me the money to disappear within the next 72 hours, then I'm going back to Detective Sanders, and telling her the truth about everything."

# Chapter 14

I couldn't reveal the truth about my black eye while I was on my double date. It wasn't even about trust since I knew Dylan and Robbie since childhood in addition to completely trusting Chuck. It wouldn't have weighed down the entire evening. There was also the issue of Chuck being a good person. I had to protect him even if I couldn't protect myself. The whole thing was laughable—even if I didn't want to admit it. It'd still be nice to find the humor in the situation years from now someday.

* * *

I walked into the kitchen hours later to make myself a glass of warm milk. It was the only thing I could think of to help me sleep. Unfortunately for me, Lucy happened to be standing there as well.

She grinned after looking up from the book her eyes were buried in seconds earlier. "Hi. How was your double date?"

If I weren't so stressed out, a part of me would've

believed she was being genuine.

I rolled my eyes. "It was fine. But please don't pretend to care about me—we both know that isn't true. You'd drive me all the way to ends of the Earth if you had your way."

Lucy shoved the book to the side. "How can you say that? Sure, we might fight, but we're still family. If you were in trouble, then I'd want to know."

"Really?" I raised an eyebrow at her. The skepticism was understandable. I couldn't remember the last time the two of had a nice interaction. And I thought about the matter for a few more moments, realizing we probably never had an honest interaction before.

"Yes. Of course. If I were lying I'd come with something a little more elaborate, don't you think?" Lucy asked.

I nibbled on the inside of my lip. Lucy had a point even if I hated admitting she was right.

I opened the fridge, attempting to find the carton of milk in the pile of rubble. Sweat fell down my face while I continued scanning the fridge. It didn't make any sense. The milk had to be in here somewhere.

Lucy shuffled over to me. "Do you need help with something?"

I turned my head. "Yeah. Where's the milk? I don't see it?"

"Elena used up all the milk earlier this evening. But we can add it to the list. I'm more than happy to pick it up tomorrow since Elena's parents will still be out of town for a few more days."

"Oh. Okay. That might be a good idea." I sobbed while my heart beat faster. The room spun in circles while I glanced around. I didn't understand it. My life was a mess. It was one truth, which lying couldn't get me out of.

"Do you want a glass of water of, Cassandra? You look overwhelmed?"

I whipped my head side to side several times. "No.

I'm fine. I'm probably just being a baby, and need a good night sleep."

"I have some alcohol stashed in my room. It might help take the edge off," she offered.

"Good for you. What do you want? A medal, or something?

She crossed her arms. "What's the matter with you? Can't you see I'm trying to be a good sister for once."

"It's a little too late for that, don't you think?"

Lucy adjusted her collar. "Okay. Now I'm really worried, Cassandra. Is that guy giving you a hard time? Let me guess. He doesn't want to cover for you anymore. All you have to do is tell me the truth."

It didn't even matter that Lucy knew the truth about Paul. I had bigger things too think about—like how I only had 48 hours to decide how to handle him or he would spill my secrets to the police.

* * *

Elena gave me a ride to school the following morning after which I told her I'd catch up to her later since wanted to have a moment or two alone with Chuck in the school parking lot.

He leaned in to kiss, pressing up my lips for a good ten seconds. "The double date was fun. Dylan and Robbie seem like cool people."

"Yeah, they are." I pulled both of my backpack straps. "I appreciate how you don't have a problem with them."

Chuck shook his head. "Why would I have a problem with them?"

"Because they're two boys in a relationship," I said. "I don't mean to get preachy or anything, but a lot of people aren't as tolerant as they claim."

He exhaled a breath. "Well, that's a shame. Anyway, we need to talk about something, Cassandra."

"Okay. Talk."

"I want to how you got that black eye. It was one thing not answer at dinner while we were out in public but now's a different story."

I averted my gaze. "I don't wanna discuss it. You wouldn't believe me even if I gave you an honest answer."

"We both know that isn't true, Cassandra. Did Paul rough you up?"

I started to sob. "Yes. He shoved me against the car and said if I didn't give him the money by tomorrow night then he'll go to the police and expose everything."

He swallowed the lump in his throat. "Thank you for telling me the truth. I know it must not have been easy for you."

Chuck had no idea. The truth wasn't a word that was in my vocabulary. Not after everything that happened with my Father. I had to be on the offensive. It was the only way for me to survive in life.

"What are you going to do?" he asked.

"I don't know. The fact is, I'm backed into a corner, and don't have a fucking clue how to get out of this ordeal."

It was nice to be at the point in my relationship with Chuck that I didn't have to worry about crying in front of him. It allowed the two of us to have a genuine element in our relationship even if I would never be good enough for him. I was broken. I couldn't deny it. Those harsh things I said to Lucy also applied to me. I was so fucked up from my childhood and early teen years that I didn't know how to have a normal life. Normal wasn't a word in my vocabulary.

* * *

I invited Paul over to the house the following afternoon since Elena's parents were still away on business, and Elena and Lucy would be at school for another couple of hours because of cheerleading practice. And the two of us were in my bedroom at the moment. I just couldn't risk a surprise. Even if I had the house to myself.

He crossed his arms. "Do you have my money?"

Money?

Fuck. Paul was a bigger brat than I was. It didn't seem possible, but it was.

I screamed, causing my voice to echo through the entire upstairs floor. I wouldn't have been surprised if a few valuables broke in the process. "No, I don't!" I exclaimed. "I'm not gonna give you the money, asshole. So, go the police. Oh, wait, you can't. You'll be an accomplice to my stunt."

Paul scoffed. "I don't care. I'll get a plea bargain, and testify against you. We both know I have enough dirt to bury you for several lifetimes."

"Just so you know, Paul, our relationship was a lie from the beginning. Even before you helped me fake my own kidnapping. You were just a method for me to escape my troubles. I could have kicked your ass to the curb anytime I wanted."

"I'm out of here." Paul darted out of the bedroom without another word.

I couldn't let him get away. It didn't take a genius to realize there was a lot at stake, so I caught up to him by the stairwell less than a minute later.

I shrilled even louder this time. "Don't walk away from me! We aren't done!"

He whirled around to face me. "Yes, we are. I'm going to the police, and your stupid ass is gonna rot in jail do you understand me?"

The lump in my throat lingered. "You can't. My life will be over."

"That's not my problem. You should've thought about that before using me."

I grabbed the letter opener on the hallway table.

Stabbing Paul was the only thing I could think of.

Paul almost turned his attention back towards the stairs. But it was too late. I mustered up all the energy I could, shoving the letter opener into stomach a good two or three times, causing him to tumble below the stairwell, and onto the floor. Something snapped. Wow. It must have been Paul's neck. The letter opener fell from my hand. Paul was dead.

I knew whom I had to call even if it would be difficult.

I grabbed my iPhone from my pocket. Then, I dialed the first number I could think of.

"Hi. I need your help," I said, panting. "There's been an accident, and you have to get here ASAP."

# Chapter 15

Paul was dead.

The whole situation hadn't sunk in yet—it couldn't be true. Things didn't work out easily in real life. I was living proof. He must have still been alive. He had to be. The wounds weren't fatal. People recovered from accidents all the time. Especially the person I hated most. It was the universe's way of sticking it to me.

I forced a gulp of air into my lungs, struggling to allow it into my body. Breathing wasn't a priority. It couldn't be. I had to figure a way to get out of this debacle.

The doorbell rang, shifting my attention to the front door. I descended the staircase, making sure not to trip over the corpse.

Corpse.

I couldn't have used that word to refer to Paul, and I shook my head. I didn't have time to debate the semantics of the situation.

I yanked open the front door, throwing a glance inside the house. "Come in."

Chuck trekked into the house, following me to the

bottom of the stairwell. His eyes moved to the floor. He didn't even clap his hand over his mouth. At least I could be glad about one thing.

He shifted his gaze back to me. "Why don't you tell me what happened?"

I coughed into my arm. "He was gonna go to the police after I invited him over to the house."

"Why did you invite him over to your house in the first place?" He glared at me for a good few seconds. I couldn't say I blamed him.

A tear rolled down my cheek. "I was hoping I could reason with him. Clearly, I was wrong."

"I need to task you a question." He sighed at me, causing his Adam's apple to throb. "But I don't think you're gonna like it."

"You can ask me. I think we know each other well enough by now. Don't you?"

"Did you bring him over here to kill him? It's okay if you did—I won't judge you. I just want to know the truth."

I glanced down at my hands for a few seconds, noticing the red stains. Some of Paul's blood must have fallen on me when I stabbed him. "No. I didn't. I swear it."

I didn't even blink. I said it with a straight face. I didn't care if he or anyone else didn't believe me. It was the God's honest truth. The situation escalated out of control just like any other tragedy.

"Do you hate me?" I asked, deciding it would be better to look at the blood stains on my hands rather than make eye contact with my boyfriend.

"I could never hate you." His jaw shook a little.

Fuck. Maybe he was more nervous than he let on.

I sobbed. "This isn't a black and white situation. He physically assaulted me, and he blackmailed me. That's illegal."

"I know, Cassandra. You don't have to remind me." He rocked his arms back and forth.

I rubbed my cheeks, not even caring about smearing Paul's blood on me. "I'm not going to the police. I'm already in enough trouble as it is. I can't be arrested for obstruction of justice and murder."

The blood returned to his face, causing it to turn redder than a stop sign. "I didn't say you should. We're on the same side."

***

The doorbell rang for a second time an hour later. I strutted over to the front door, gasping at the people on the front steps.

I frowned. "What are you guys doing here? No offense or anything, but it's not exactly a good time to chat. Can we pick this up later?"

"It's okay," said a voice. "I called them, and told them you needed their help."

I cocked my head, facing Chuck. "Have you lost your mind?"

Lucy grunted. "You should invite us in. We wouldn't want to draw unwanted attention."

Robbie snickered. "Yeah. I hate to admit it, but Lucy has a point."

"Fine." I gesticulated at Elena, Lucy, Robbie, and Dylan to come inside. Then, I locked the door behind them. I couldn't afford another surprise. It was bad enough Chuck went behind my back.

We made our way to the crime scene.

Elena was the only to scream. It made sense. Robbie, Dylan, and Lucy were stronger than Elena.

Steam would have seeped out of Elena's head if she were a cartoon character. "What the hell is going on, Cassandra?" she demanded. "You better start talking. Otherwise we're gonna go to the police."

Lucy smacked her hand over her mouth. "Fuck. He really was blackmailing you, wasn't he?"

I nodded at Lucy. The words couldn't fall out of mouth at the moment. Besides, I needed to conserve my energy and come up with a new plan.

"Paul helped me fake the kidnapping story. But when my father died in the fire I used that as an excuse to come back to town. It didn't matter if it was dangerous. Paul was starting to grow tired of living on the run. The only problem was Detective Sanders wasn't that stupid. She wasn't buying my story. I begged Paul to confess to get Sanders off my back. So, he did. But I wasn't about to let him go down for a crime he didn't commit. So, I broke him out of his holding cell since he hadn't been transferred to the prison yet." I took a brief pause in my rant, allowing myself to catch my breath. With any luck, I would have been there talking till the end of time.

"But then he came back to town after I told him Detective Sanders had proof I wasn't kidnapped. I tried to get him to come forward again, but he wouldn't. I can't say I blame him 100 percent. The lie would have been hard to pull off. But then he blackmailed me for 10 million dollars so he could spend the rest of his life on the run and pretend to be wealthy since there was still technically a warrant out for his arrest. But I didn't want to pay him off even though he was going to go to the police and try and cut a deal," I continued. "And just so you know, he was the one who gave me a black eye after shoving me against his car…"

Elena screamed even louder this time. "I can't believe you, Cassandra. You killed someone."

"You could lose the righteous attitude, Elena," I spat. "We both know you aren't one to talk."

"And what's that supposed to mean?" Elena asked.

My head swayed back and forth. "Forget it."

Elena glared at me. "No matter what the details of the situation are, you still lied to fake your kidnapping. Do you have anything to say for yourself?"

"My father physically abused me as a kid. That's

how I got this." I rolled up my sleeve, revealing my scar. "He burned me with a cigarette. Ask Lucy. He abused her too."

Elena looked at Lucy.

"Yes, it's true," Lucy said. "Our father was a monster. As much as I might hate my sister for leaving me behind, I know I can't blame her."

Robbie rubbed his cross necklace. "What do you want to do, Cassandra?"

"I want to get rid of the body. Let's drag it to the woods and burn it." My throat tightened while I struggled to take a breath. Wow. I'd be lucky if I didn't have a heart attack.

"That isn't gonna be enough," Elena said.

It took everything I had not to yell at her. "What do you mean?" I demanded.

"I'm not trying to be mean," Lucy stammered. "But we should get some bleach and wipe the stairs and carpets."

"Fine," I said. "You can be in charge of that while I look for gasoline and matches, and then drag his body out to the woods with everyone else."

Lucy rolled her eyes. "Okay. Have it your way. I guess it would be too easy for you to clean up your own crime scene."

* * *

Elena, Chuck, Dylan, Robbie, and I returned from the woods a couple of hours later.

The smell of bleach hit my nose, making me smile. It was impressive. The blood was really gone in addition to how that Lucy got rid of the mop already.

Lucy exited the kitchen, glancing at me. "It's taken care of. If anyone asks, we did some cleaning."

"Wow." I snickered. "It looks like that I'm not the only who knows how to lie."

* * *

Chuck, Dylan, and Robbie left hours later before Lucy eventually walked into the living room with a bottle.

She clipped closer and closer, arriving at the couch in a matter of seconds. She handed me the bottle after sitting on the couch.

"Here," she said. "You need it more than me."

I grabbed the bottle from her. It was Jose Cuervo. "Thanks."

I gulped down some of the tequila before opening my mouth again. I looked my sister in the eye. "We need to talk about something, Lucy."

"Of course. You know you can talk about anything with me." She moved around on the couch, getting comfortable.

I ran my fingers through my hair. It didn't even matter if my hands weren't shaking. Any distraction was welcome even if was a vanity thing. "No matter what our differences have been over the years, I want to remind you that nobody can know about what we did tonight. Just remember I still know what you did."

"I'm not an idiot. I wouldn't do that to you. Not after everything that happened."

I handed her the bottle. "Here. You're an accessory to murder. You need this as much as I do."

"No. It's fine. I meant when I said. The bottle's all yours."

I put the bottle on the table.

A scorching sensation shot through my stomach. "I know it sounds awful, but I have to say this," I said. "I don't regret what I did. Yes, I am sorry it came to this. But I did what I had to do just like he did. The only difference between us is that I'm still standing."

Paul wasn't the only thing that collapsed. Whether I wanted to admit it or not, Paul was my only link to lying about the kidnapping thing. So, I was on my own now. And I'd just hope Detective Sanders wouldn't realize Paul was "missing," because it was the last thing I needed. She was already hot on my trail as it was. All it took for her was to ask one question and the whole thing would blow up. That's the nature of life even if people didn't want to admit it. Everything was subjected to imploding at a moment's notice, which was a reason to watch my step. If I wasn't careful, then my life would be over before it began.

# Chapter 16

The events surrounding Paul's death would remain etched in my brain till my last dying breath. It couldn't be helped. Damn. This was what murderers must have felt like.

But I wasn't a murderer.

People weren't always born wicked. True evil was made, not born. Even if my own lies got me into my current debacle.

It didn't matter if I couldn't say verbalize the point. Elena, Chuck, Dylan, Robbie, Lucy and I would be bounded together for life because of the murder. There was no way around it. If it wasn't such a tragedy, then it would have been poetic that all of our fates were sealed to each other.

The only question was if we would turn on each other. We couldn't. It didn't matter if we would have eventual differences someday. The whole operation would fall apart if we did. And I couldn't afford that to happen.

Not now.

Everything would have been for nothing.

* * *

Someone tapped my shoulder the next morning at school after I gulped down a drink at the water fountain.

I whipped around to see who it was. I would have been glad to see Elena under any other circumstances, but not today. I wasn't an idiot. I was there when Elena vocalized her concerns the previous evening.

Elena clicked her lips together. "We need to talk, Cassandra."

"I thought we said we weren't gonna talk about it." I tucked a lock of hair behind my ear.

"Plans change. I held back last night. But not after everything that happened."

A lump lingered in my throat. "What are you talking about?"

"I think you just wanna drag us down to Hell with you."

I raised an eyebrow at her. "What are you talking about that? That's bullshit."

She tugged at the sides of her jacket, flicking her hair behind her neck. "I think you called us there because you wanted to avoid the blame. We are now co-conspirators."

Elena stretched this one. Nobody could deny I needed help even if I was smart. Getting away with murder wasn't amateur. There was no way I could have pulled it off myself. It had to be a team effort even if Elena didn't want to admit it.

"Did you forget that no matter what you think of me, I'm still implicated in everything?" I asked.

"Doesn't matter. We are in this debacle because you made a mess of your personal life."

I grabbed Elena by her arm, dragging her to an empty corridor.

She pushed my arm off her. "Let go of me!"

I locked my arms together, pressing them against my chest. "You heard Lucy. I didn't make up the abuse story."

"That's what you claim." Elena paused for a moment. "But for all we know, you blackmailed her into going along with your story."

I stood on my tip toes, towering above Elena. "In case you forgot, there are some things I know about your past."

She recoiled. "This isn't the time or place to bring that up."

"Yeah, it is. I stuck by you after what happened. And you should do the same for me."

"Are you threatening me?" Elena asked.

I shook my head in a vigorous fashion. "No. I wouldn't say that."

Elena's rude behavior was another thing that happened even if it shouldn't. I couldn't talk my way out of this situation as much as I wanted to. It was foolish to think something so big could happen and there wouldn't be any consequences.

A bell screeched. I'd have to go to first period whether I wanted to or not.

Elena darted off in the opposite direction.

"You have to keep your word because last night proves how far I'll go. If you burry me, I'll bury you," I bellowed. It didn't even matter if she hadn't turned her head to look back at me. It needed to be said.

* * *

Chuck and I flocked to the cafeteria a few hours later while we held hands. It was nice in a way, because I could pretend to do a normal teenage thing even though I committed murder less than 24 hours earlier.

He cocked his head. "Everything okay, Cassandra? You seem quieter than usual."

I squeezed his hand. "Elena spoke to me this morning. She thinks I just wanted everyone there so I could place the blame. I couldn't believe her. The nerve of that girl. Especially after everything I did for her."

Chuck let go of my hand, then blocked my path. "What are you talking about?"

"Forget it. Doesn't matter."

"Are you worried Elena is gonna rat you out?" Chuck asked.

"No. But that doesn't mean she shouldn't be watched."

"Why don't you want to tell me what you know about Elena?"

I averted my gaze, deciding to look at somebody's student council poster. Not that it mattered or anything. It wasn't like I was going to vote for the person. I didn't even need to glance at the poster to know it was another anonymous loser. The school was filled with them, including Elena.

I couldn't deny Chuck had a good point. I could have told him what I knew about Elena. It was better this way, though. Chuck shouldn't have been involved in anymore of my dramatic situations than he needed to be. Chuck was pure. Protecting his innocence was the one thing I had to be sure of. And I was. I didn't have any doubt in my mind. Not even a little.

It wasn't even about having a pity party for myself. I was lucky to have Chuck in my life. He accepted me. It was rather refreshing. Everyone else only talked to me out of habit whereas Chuck and I had a genuine connection even if there had been a few ups and downs since we first met.

I couldn't be surprised. Manipulation came with a price. There were only so many factors I could control. It was basic math.

But there was still the lingering question of how to handle Elena. The whole situation was an enigma. Getting my way was key even if she couldn't see it like that. Elena would roll over someday. She had to. We survived much worse.

* * *

I descended the home staircase a couple of mornings later, only to find Elena's mom in the kitchen. I also gasped at what rocked back and forth in Mrs. Brook's hand. It was my tequila bottle from the previous evening.

I coughed. "What's going on, Mrs. Brooks?"

"I found this bottle when I was in your room gathering your laundry the other day," she said, continuing to hold the bottle.

"Look, Mrs. Brooks, don't get me wrong. I'm thankful for everything you've done for me and Lucy, but if you expect an apology for underage drinking, then you'll be disappointed."

She sighed, not even bothering to roll her eyes. "If you're gonna drink, you should at least do it when my husband or I are home. That way, we can keep an eye on you."

I nodded. "Sure. You have to believe, I'm not using it for a crux or anything. I mean, the cliché is true. You're only young once. I deserve to have a little fun. Don't you *watch Gossip Girl?*"

In retrospect, I was lucky. Mrs. Brooks could have been a lot angrier with me for underage drinking. But she wasn't. I could only begin to imagine what my father would have done to me if he caught me drinking. He probably would have burned me with his cigarette or locked me in the basement for an evening without dinner. I wasn't sure what was worse. Being burned with a cigarette was painful. On the other hand, being locked in a basement offered a claustrophobic element. There was nothing like feeling trapped—the thought daunted me.

But it wouldn't happen.

Not again.

My father was dead thanks to Lucy, which meant I would be able to rest easy about one thing.

Every event blurred with the next. That was the problem when I was involved in something so larger than life. The even takes on a life of its own until it consumes you. But it wouldn't happen to me. I was the exception, not the rule. I was Cassandra Fucking Jenkins, after all. Bad things didn't happen to me. They couldn't.

That was a lie.

They had. But I could at least pretend to live in my bubble of denial. After all, delusions of grandeur and acute psychosis were comforting even if they were unhealthy. It was a survival mechanism for me. And that was okay. It was just another thing to help me through the day.

* * *

I couldn't sleep that night. I couldn't say I was surprised. People could still suffer from post-traumatic stress disorder even if they didn't go to war. I should know. It started long before the murder and subsequent cover up.

I didn't even bother fumbling around on my bed. It wouldn't do me any good.

It also didn't help that I could hear the splattering of rain from outside. The splashing sounds got louder with each passing second.

But there was one thing I could do.

I closed my eyes even if I couldn't fall asleep.

My mind drifted back to around the time I first met Paul as we had several encounters in town before he worked up the courage to ask me on a date.

I was balancing my iPhone between my ear and shoulder while I shuffled through my purse as I was about to enter the Starbucks on Main Street.

Most people wouldn't have been bothered to open a door for a complete stranger.

But not Paul. He was different.

I mouthed, "thank you" at him even though I was still on my phone. He nodded back at me, causing me to smile.

Opening a door for a complete stranger didn't define his whole personality. However, it did reveal he was more than an anonymous nobody. It was a small gesture.

I would concede it.

But Paul's politeness still mattered to me.

Tears came to my eyes while the rain picked up. Paul was dead, and it was all my fault. It didn't matter if I didn't go to jail. I was gonna have live with that for the rest of my life.

But he wasn't a monster. Not completely. I shaped the person he became because I didn't just physically kill him. I also killed the good inside him. So, yeah. I wouldn't hesitate to remember Paul as the person he once was versus the person he became. After all, it would be nice if I were remembered that way.

Paul mattered. He just wasn't made to live as his perfect self in an imperfect world. Really, it was tragic. But at least I could take solace in how he was free from my lies now since I needed to shake the scent of burning flesh from my mind.

# Chapter 17

I stood in the kitchen several days later after school one day. I brought the mug to my lips, allowing the steam to press up against my mouth. A headline popped out at me from the muted TV that somebody must have accidentally left on: **Body Found Burnt in the Woods Behind "Kidnapped Girl's" Home**

I put my mug on the counter, shoving it to the side. I had to hear the news. I grabbed the remote, turning the volume louder than I needed to. It must have been one of my overreacting impulses.

"A burnt body was found in the woods of Kidnapped Girls" home a.k.a. Cassandra Jenkins after an anonymous person gave the police a tip. At this time, they haven't released the name of the victim as they are still running tests to identify the body. The police revealed they are actively investigated, and nobody has been named as a person of interest at the time in an official press release, which was released by the Clarksville Police Department," said the news anchor.

I shouldn't have been surprised. My life was proof

that it only took one thing to happen for something to fall apart. I could only begin to wonder who gave the police the anonymous tip. It seemed unlikely it would have been one of my friends because they would be incriminating themselves. Although the people I knew best were the most capable of betraying me. It was the one thing I learned from my English classes over the years.

I bit my lip, leaving a metallic taste in my mouth.

Detective Sanders would probably be working the case even if I didn't want to admit it. Her sharpness was something I could no longer ignore no matter how hard I tried.

But she hadn't caught me yet.

It might not have been much, but it was something. My determination would be my salvation in the long run. There was no doubt about it even if it didn't help me that even the news labeled me, "Kidnapped Girl." It was nauseating despite the saying that there was no so such thing as bad publicity. Bullshit. I was already under a big microscope, and the scrutiny didn't need to increase.

I would find a way out of my current debacle. I found a way out of Paul blackmailing me, after all.

*** 

Chuck, Robbie, Dylan, Elena, Lucy, and I gathered in my bedroom half an hour later despite the awkwardness of the whole situation. After all, the cover up was the easy part. It was the aftermath that mattered more.

Elena crossed her arms. "What are we doing here, Cassandra? Don't you think you've wasted enough of our time already?"

I snickered. "You live at the same house as me, meaning your attendance didn't require much effort."

Lucy turned her head, allowing herself to face me. "It was about the news, wasn't it?"

Robbie put his hands on his hips. "What news?

Did something happen?"

Lucy's exhaled a long breath. "Do you want to tell them, or shall I?"

"I'll tell them." I took my hands to my jacket, straightening it. It didn't matter if I was neck deep in shit. Everything had to be perfect even if was going to be dragged down to hell. "Somebody sent an anonymous tip to the police about where Paul's body was buried."

"You've gotta be kidding me. That was just what we needed." Dylan scratched his neck for a second.

Elena scoffed at me. "You did this, didn't you? You're gonna find a way to throw us all under the bus to save yourself."

I ran my fingers through my hair. "That's bullshit, and you know it. I'm already on the detective's radar as it is. So, despite what you think of me, it wouldn't be in my best interest to throw you all under a bus."

Lucy smacked her tongue against her lips, messing up some of her lipstick in the process. "You really have a lot of nerve, Elena—you're in it just like the rest of us. If you ask me, it's time to get on board."

Elena shot Lucy a venomous glare. "When did you become Cassandra's cheerleader?"

Lucy averted her gaze to the Green Day poster in my room, remaining silent.

Chuck grinned. "Did the news say anything else? Do they know who it is?"

I swallowed the lump in my throat. "No. Forensic tests are still pending."

"Look. There still time to go to Sanders and explain the situation." A bead of sweat rolled down Elena's face. "We don't have to go down for this."

"You really are delusional, Elena. Maybe you should see a shrink," I said.

A silence ensued for a couple minutes while everyone refused to look each other in the eye.

"I have to ask. Did one of you go to police, and

give them an anonymous tip?" I said, coughing into my sleeve.

They all shook their heads at me.

I glanced at Chuck, Elena, Lucy, Dylan, and Robbie. They weren't even blinking or laughing. They must have been telling the truth. Even Elena. I didn't know what was worse. Having a friend betray me or realizing there was someone else out there that wanted to take me down since that meant things were beyond my control.

I didn't need to tell my friends that someone else was after me. We had enough problems as it was. One more problem would push us over the edge. It didn't take a genius to figure that out.

Not knowing who was after me would probably drive me crazy even if there was nothing I could do about the situation. It was another thing I had to live—whether I liked it or not.

* * *

Chuck and I walked to first period the following morning at school while holding hands.

He sighed. "Are you sure you're okay about everything?"

"Yeah. I'm fine. It's just one more thing that happened to me."

"If it were I'd be on edge," Chuck said. "I can't even begin to imagine what you're thinking."

The matter simmered in my mind for almost a minute. It would have been nice to be able to tell Chuck the whole truth since I was trying to be a better person. But there was still the issue of not knowing if I could trust him or not.

"There's something I have to tell you," I said while we turned the corner in the hallway.

He beamed his eyes. "Okay. And what's that? Don't tell me there's another murder we have to cover up?"

"That's not funny."

"You're right, I should know better. I'm sorry. I just thought you of all people would appreciate the humor in such a macabre situation."

"Anyway, I think somebody is after me that isn't a part of the group."

"What did you just say?" he asked.

I came to an abrupt halt in the hallway. "Yeah. I'm serious. I believed everyone last night. I don't think anyone of us went to the police."

He inhaled a breath. "I'm gonna ask you a question, but I don't want you to be mad at me."

"Okay. But you know you can ask me anything. I'm an open book."

"Did you go to the police?" Chuck whispered in a tone I almost couldn't hear.

I whipped my head back and forth. "No, I didn't. I swear it. I have the most to lose."

He forced a smile. "No need to worry. I was just asking you a question. It wasn't like I actually thought Elena was right."

"There's something else you need to know. It has to do when I first came back to town." A tear rolled down my face. Some things scared even me. "Somebody sent me a note stating they knew my kidnapping story was a lie."

Chuck quirked an eyebrow. "Let me guess. You think it's the same person who told the police about the body?"

I nodded. "Yeah. I do. I know it sounds crazy, but it has to be true."

"Can the police even get DNA off a burnt body?"

"Yes. They can." I ran my fingers through my hair, deciding a ponytail was my best option. After all, there was enough going on as it was—I didn't need anything else to get in my way, even a loose strand of hair.

He grabbed my hand. "Well, you know I'm here

for you, whatever you need."

"Thanks." I leaned in, giving him a quick kiss on the lips.

***

I knocked on Lucy's bedroom door hours later in the evening.

"Come in," said Lucy from behind the door.

I shuffled into the bedroom, discovering Lucy spread out on her bed while she sifted through one of her magazines.

"Do you mind if I ask you for something?"

She closed the magazine before looking up at me. "You know you can ask me anything."

Sweat trickled down my face. "Do you have any booze? I could use a drink."

Lucy plopped up from the bed. "Of course. You know I'm here to help."

She walked over to her drawer, pulling out a bottle. She handed it to me a minute later. "Here you go. I hope Jack Daniel's is okay."

"It's fine." I took the bottle from her, gulping down a good third of the bottle before giving it back to Lucy. "Thanks. You don't know how much I needed that."

"Don't mention it. I meant what I said the other day. I want things to be good between us."

"There's something I need to know." I took a long paused before barreling along with the rest of my train of thought. "Why are you helping me? I mean, I'm not trying to look a gift horse in the mouth or anything, but I'd be lying if I said our relationship hasn't been complicated over the years."

Lucy glanced at me, giving me a good look over. "I know. But if you go down, I go down. It's as simple as that. Believe what you want, but we're on the same team.

It just took me time to realize that."

I didn't have time to debate her statement. A ringing sound rolled through the air. It must have been the doorbell.

"I'll get that." I trekked out of the room in a matter of seconds before descending the stairwell.

It didn't take a genius to realize who was at the front door no matter how difficult things were at the moment.

I opened the front door, then masked my contempt at who stood on the front porch. "What are you doing here?"

She clenched her jaw. "The forensics tests are in. The dental records match Paul's."

"What are you saying?" I didn't take my eyes off Detective Sanders. Not even for a second.

"The jig is up, Cassandra. Paul's dead, and we'd like to bring you in for questioning." Her grin widened.

"Elena's parents aren't home at the moment, which means you can't talk to me."

"Fine." Her chest contracted and expanded several times. "But I want you to march your ass down to the police station the second one of them gets home. Do you understand me?"

I closed the door on Detective Sanders, not even giving any thought to accidentally being rude. The bitch deserved what was coming to her.

It couldn't be true.

Everything was falling apart, and if I didn't act quickly, I'd be going down.

# Chapter 18

"**L**ucy, get down here now!" My voice echoed, vibrating through the entire house.

It was the loudest I ever screamed. Detective Sanders hadn't even been gone for five minutes. It didn't matter, though. Something had to be done about Bitch Sanders. She took up enough of my time as it was. She was worse than an insect. Insects could be killed with one swat. Jane on the other hand was different. It was no secret she was determined to make my life a living hell. It was a shame she had nothing better to do than to harass a teenager. It was disgusting. The bad guys lurked in the background, wreaking havoc while the police investigated all the wrong people.

Footsteps scraped the ground floor before my sister scurried over to my location by the front door.

"Something wrong?" Lucy asked.

I pouted. "Detective Sanders was here again."

She shot me a glance. "I'm sorry. Is there something I can do for you?"

I nodded. "I want you to hit me."

"Excuse me? Have you lost your mind?"

"No, I haven't. I need you to do this because I'm going to tell Elena's mom that Detective Sanders punched me."

"You don't think that's a risk? We're already in it deep as it is."

I shook my head. "I need to turn the tables, and get the spotlight off me. If people think Sanders hit, then she can be sued for police brutality."

"If you say so. I just hope you know what you're doing." Lucy twirled a strand of hair, wrapping it around her index finger.

"What are you waiting for. Just do it already…"

It didn't matter if it'd hurt. It had to be done. Detective Sanders needed to know there wasn't anything I wouldn't do to vanquish her from my life. My age didn't matter. I was a force to be reckoned with. There wasn't any scheme too twisted for me. Maybe I watched too much television. Or maybe I just did what I needed to survive. The only difference between me and other people was I wasn't afraid to do the difficult things.

Mrs. Brooks darted into the kitchen half an hour later, clapping her hand over my mouth when she saw me. "Shit. What happened to you?"

Tears pricked my eyes. "Detective Sanders stopped by. She punched me when I refused to go to the police station even though you and your husband weren't home. Don't you see it? She won't stop till she decimates me. You have to help me, Mrs. Brooks."

She raised an eyebrow at me. "Are you for real?"

I swallowed the burning sensation in my mouth, as if I just downed an entire bottle of vodka in one sitting. "Yes, she hit me. I swear it."

Mrs. Brooks grabbed my arm, taking me out of the kitchen. "Come on!"

"Where are we going?" I asked.

"To the police station." She paused for a moment.

"We're going to give this lady a piece of my mind."

It was nice. Detective Sanders was gonna get a taste of her own medicine. I had something she didn't. A grownup on my side. Mrs. Brooks believed me and that was all that mattered.

* * *

We arrived at the police station twenty minutes later. The universe was on our side this evening as we didn't even have to look that hard for Detective Sanders. She was in the lobby, heading towards the elevator.

"We need to talk, Detective Sanders," said Mrs. Brooks.

She turned around. "Oh my. What happened to your eye, Cassandra?"

I sobbed. "Are you kidding me, bitch? You were the one who hit me when I wouldn't come to the police station without Mrs. Brooks or her husband."

Mrs. Brooks shot Detective Sanders a dirty look. "You have a lot of nerve. Don't you know you aren't supposed to talk to a minor without a guardian present, or did you go to clown college?"

Detective Sanders snickered. "That's rich. Can't you see that she's playing you?"

I turned to Mrs. Brooks. "She's the one playing you. She's been harassing me for weeks. You have no idea how many sleepless nights I've endured over the whole situation."

She elevated an eyebrow. "Did that really happen, Detective Sanders?"

Detective Sanders didn't say anything. Some things were beyond words, even for her. What a shocker! She must have been dying on the inside. A teenager was playing the game better than she was. It was laughable. Detective Sanders didn't even know what hit her.

Elena's mom pointed her finger at Sanders. "If

you even so much as think about talking to Cassandra without my husband or I, I'll take you for everything you're worth. Do you understand me?"

Detective Sanders glared at me. "You must be proud of yourself. I'll give you one thing. You're a better liar than I realized. You should win an Oscar."

Wow. Even Detective Sanders conceded I was a good liar. It was refreshing to know I had her beat at something. I couldn't be surprised. She was a cop, after all. Being able to tell who was lying and who was telling the truth was how she made a living.

Mrs. Brooks locked her arms together. "Are you charging Cassandra with anything?"

She exhaled a long breath. "Not at the moment. But as you know, homicide investigations tend to change. So, she might be in an orange jumpsuit sooner than she thinks."

"See!" I cried. "Don't you get it, Mrs. Brooks? She's obsessed with me because she's too lazy to actually do her job."

Mrs. Brooks suppressed her smile. "Yes, you're right. And it's something I'll tell my lawyer."

"You do that," Detective Sanders said. She didn't wait for Mrs. Brooks and I to say anything. She wobbled away in the opposite direction.

I expelled a long breath. At least I would be able to sleep tonight. It was something to be happy about it. The war wasn't over yet, though. Today's solution was only temporary. I would have to come up with a more permanent solution for Sanders. The only question was what it would be.

* * *

I attempted to do some homework later in the evening even though I was interrupted an hour into my efforts.

"You have a lot of nerve, you know that," roared a

voice.

I lifted my gaze off my textbook, plopping myself up from my chair. "Good to see you, Elena. Long time no talk."

"You really crossed the line this time. I hope you know that."

I swayed my head back and forth a couple of times. "What are you talking about?"

She smacked her arms together. "I overheard you and Lucy talking earlier. Are you really stupid enough to lie to the police again? You could get arrested for filing a false police report."

I stepped forward. "First of all, we didn't even file the report. I just did what I needed to do get Sanders off my back. You of all people should realize that."

"No offense or anything, but I'd prefer it if you left my mom out of our mess."

I put my hands on my hips. "You can't tell me what to do."

Elena cackled, pricking the hairs on my back. "Watch me. For far too long, you've been bossing everyone around. That ends today."

I rolled my eyes. "You wanna know what I think? I think you just have a guilty conscious about that Spring Break, and you are using this situation to take your anger out on me."

"That's bullshit, and you know it. The two situations are different."

"Not really," I said. "You forget I know how to read people. You can't get anything past me. At least, I'm trying to protect everyone. That's more than I can say for you. Now get the hell out of my room."

"Fine. With pleasure." She shuffled towards the exit before cocking her head to look back at me for a moment. "But just so you know, Cassandra, after this fake kidnapping-murder cover up situation is over, I don't ever want you to bring up that Spring Break again, do you hear me?"

* * *

I ate lunch with Chuck the following day outside at one of the tables in front of the school's main entrance. I glanced up at the sky for a moment. Beams of sunlight poked through the clouds, shining down on us. The warmth from the touch spread through my whole body. It would probably be one of the last few warm days left. Winter was coming whether people wanted to admit it or not."

Chuck took his eyes off his tuna fish sandwich, deciding to glance up at me. "How have you been?"

"Okay. But unfortunately, Detective Sanders showed up the other day. I took care of her, though. I had Lucy punch me and told Elena's mom it was Detective Sanders that punched me."

"Oh okay. I didn't realize we were still aboard the crazy train express." He took a bite of his food before reaching for his water bottle.

I didn't have time to debate the subtext of his, "oh okay." That was a problem for another time. I had to focus on keeping Chuck on my side. It wouldn't be difficult. He wasn't as black and white as Elena, which meant he saw the world like I did. It was kind of refreshing since Elena's moral behavior was starting to get irritating.

It wasn't annoying to have to tell Chuck the truth about my latest lie. Chuck was a trustworthy person. He proved that a thousand times before. There was no question about it. It still would have been nice to know what he thought about me. I had to be more than just a liar to him. He stayed with me despite my imperfections. It meant something even if I didn't exactly know what it was at the moment. At least I wasn't afraid to show somebody the real me. That was positive. The wall had to come down sometime even if only for a second.

Chuck was turning into a better boyfriend than

Paul. There was no doubt about it. It took reflection to realize what I had with Paul was a terrible dysfunctional relationship. It was a miracle I lasted as long as I did. Chuck would never do what Paul did. It only took one minute to realize it—he didn't have the guts. And that was a good thing. Chuck was pure; Paul wasn't. It didn't take long to wrap my head around the issue.

The comforting thing was I extracted myself from the situation before it was too late.

* * *

I returned home from school hours later, finding a woman on the front steps.

Except it wasn't Detective Sanders, any neighbor or adult acquaintance.

My heart beat increased, shooting blood through my veins while I struggled to find the words to speak. "Can I help you?"

"Yeah," she said. "Detective Sanders told me where to find you." She paused for a sec. "I know you killed my son."

# Chapter 19

I crossed my arms. "No offense, lady, but that's conjecture. You have no proof that I did what you think I did."

She flipped her hair over her shoulders, allowing the beams of sunlight to reveal all the shades of her salt and pepper hair. "I don't need proof. If Detective Sanders thinks you killed my son, then you did."

My nostrils flared "Paul told me about you. He said you kicked him out of the house when he was 16. Is that true?"

The lady didn't say anything. Apparently, she inherited Detective Sanders's taste in remaining silent.

"You know what I think? I think you need to get off my property before I call the cops."

She hissed. "Go ahead. It's not like they would believe you. You're nothing but a stupid girl."

"How dare you! You don't know a damn thing about my life."

"I know enough," she said. "Besides, did you know Paul called me a couple of days before he died?"

I shot her a venomous glare. "Listen, lady, it's not my problem you've got unresolved issues with your son. Maybe if you had been a better mother, then you wouldn't be in your current predicament. But no. You were a terrible mother."

She raced over to where I stood at the moment. The distinct odor of whatever mouthwash she used even prickled my skin. "Somebody should teach you some respect."

"Respect is for losers. Now go to therapy like a normal person. At least a therapist has to pretend to care unlike everyone else in your life."

It was too late.

She smacked me across the face, leaving a stinging sensation. I took my hand to the spot where she hit me, feeling the wound. I huffed at the woman before whipping something out from my bag.

"Get off my property," I said, placing my hands on the trigger of my gun.

"Tell me something. Do you even have a permit for your gun?"

I clicked my lips together. "Doesn't matter. Last time I checked, you were trespassing on private property, which means you're the one in the wrong."

"Very well. But you haven't seen the last of me."

I went inside without looking back at the woman. Some people had a lot of nerve. She had no right to trespass on private property regardless who was right or wrong. The woman was as crazy as Detective Sanders and that was saying something. If only they were bisexual or gay—they would make the perfect match for each other.

Detective Sanders.

That brought me to my next problem. She contacted Paul's mom. There was no doubt about it. But it was okay. I dealt with Paul's mom. One look at my gun sent the lady running away in the opposite direction. It was rather amusing. There was still the issue of her being unstable. I couldn't ignore it. She was also a problem I'd have to deal with sooner rather than later. The perfect solution would come to me. I'd just have to give it time. Even if it was the one thing I didn't have.

* * *

I sat on the park bench on Main Street the next morning before school. The wind howled, picking up the leaves. The hues of red, orange, and brown stole my attention. There was nothing like the crisp scent of fall. Fall would have been nicer if it didn't lead to winter. Oh well. Winter was inevitable like everything else in life, which meant it didn't take a genius to realize it was also my least favorite season. After all, winter wasn't as fashionable as spring, summer, and fall.

The woman approached me, getting closer and closer.

"I was surprised to get your call," said the woman, brushing her pants off when she sat down.

"I didn't have a choice, Detective Sanders. You have a lot of damn nerve, you know that? You had no right to send Paul's mother after me."

She bit her lip. "I did no such thing. I merely told her the facts of the case. It's not my fault she's a little mentally unbalanced."

"Forgive me for being blunt, but I thought it was time we cleared the air."

She gesticulated at me. "By all means. If you have something to say, then I'm interested in hearing it."

I cackled. It didn't matter if this was no time to act arrogant. The bitch needed to know who was in charge. "You and I both know you are never gonna arrest me."

"Is that so?"

I nodded. "Yes. It is. We both know if you make one move against me then I'll have Elena's mom slap with you a police brutality lawsuit so fast it'll make your head spin."

"I'd love to see you try."

I rolled my sleeves up. "Don't test me, lady."

"Since this is an off the record chat, that means you don't have to worry about me using your response against you in court," Detective Sanders said. "I want to know something. Did you kill Paul?"

The grin vanished from my face. "Yes, I killed him. And I'd do it again. He was blackmailing me about giving him enough money to live on the run forever. So, congrats, Detective! You were right about the fake kidnapping story.

"Well, at least you gave me an honest answer." She pushed a lock of her hair out of the way. "That's something I suppose."

"But there's something you don't know," I said. "Paul got violent with me. He shoved me against the car."

Her jaw dropped a little. "Oh. I see. I can't imagine what that must have felt like for you."

I tapped my feet on the ground. "As you can see, this crime was a crime of passion. Not premeditated murder."

"Why not go to the police?" Her eyes widened at me.

I averted my gaze, choosing to look at squirrel climbing up a tree instead. "No one would ever believe me. The truth wasn't on my side."

She sipped her coffee. "I see. Well, anyway, there's something you need to know, Cassandra. I won't use what you told me today against you. But I'm still going to build a case against you."

"What?" The blood rushed through my entire body at the moment, almost causing blisters to form in my veins. "I thought if I told the truth then the whole matter would just be forgotten."

Her head swooshed back and forth. "I'm afraid not. I'm going to make your life a living hell. Just you wait."

I got up from the bench, continuing to make eye contact with her. "Well, then I hope you know that when you finally do charge me I'll be ready to file that false police report."

Her nostrils flared. "You don't have to put on an act for Elena's mom. She isn't around. We both know you lied."

"Doesn't matter. I have the support of Elena's mom, while you have no one."

It was nice to be able to confront Detective Sanders no matter how risky the endeavor seemed. I had to fight fire with fire—I wasn't some weak little girl to be pushed around. The days of playing victim were long gone. It didn't matter who my enemy was. I would only hope Elena didn't require the same amount of venom as my battle with Detective Sanders. No matter. Everything would be dealt with. The important thing was Sanders knew I was on to her. I wasn't about to play stupid by worrying about showing my hand too soon. That would get me nowhere. People like Sanders needed to be dealt with right away. There was no debate to be had about the matter—Sanders was the enemy. It was as simple as that. There was nothing redeemable about the woman. She actually said it out loud. She was going to make my life a living hell. It was despicable.

But if there was one thing I learned it was good things came to those who least deserved them. And fortunately for me, I was a sinner. I knew it. Detective Sanders knew it and so did the rest of the world. Elena was also a sinner even if she would never admit it.

It wasn't like our Spring Break trip to Mexico could be forgotten. It was the kind of thing that stuck with you long after the events were over.

Mexico was nothing compared to the events in present day. Elena knew it too. It was actually kind of obvious. Elena was more inclined to behave dramatically then she cared to admit.

* * *

I tossed and turned in my bed hours later, failing to fall sleep that evening. Mexico must have been on my mind more than I cared to admit.

* * *

Elena and I came back to the roof of the night club we snuck into with fake I.D.s, only to find the guy we'd been talking to wasn't there.

We searched the entire roof, unable to find the person.

Elena pulled at the side of her head, almost taking her hair off in the process. "Where's Julio?"

I shrugged. "He obviously isn't here."

She started to sob a little. "I knew we shouldn't have left him alone. He was pretty dramatic."

I jabbed her in the shoulder. "When are you going to learn to lighten up, Elena? This is a vacation, now start realizing it."

"Excuse me for caring." She continued glancing around.

She smacked her hand over her mouth a minute later.

It wasn't long before I walked over to her. "What is it?"

She pointed at the ground with her free hand. My eyes zoomed in below us, discovering the man that was on the ground.

"He must have fallen to the ground since he was drunk and acting foolish." I wiped a tear from my eye.

Elena quirked an eyebrow at me. "Are you really gonna blame the incident on him?"

I drew in several long breaths. "No. I'm just saying

that it wasn't anyone's fault. It was an accident. There was nothing we could have done for him."

"Come on! We have to get out of here!" Elena tugged at my arm, causing me to drop the drinks I was holding.

* * *

Elena was kind of being a drama queen.

It was still an accident even if I didn't enjoy the fact somebody was dead—we hadn't set out to harm Julio. Although Elena did have a point about one thing since we shouldn't have left him by himself. Drunks needed to be supervised—it was basic logic.

I got out of bed. There was no problem with admitting I wouldn't be able to sleep tonight. I descended the staircase, making my way to the kitchen. I grabbed the coffee pot, deciding I might as well be alert if it wasn't going to be able to sleep. The contents flowed into the mug in no time. It wasn't long before the half and half splashed its way into the cup. I took a spoon from the drawer, then stirred my coffee.

I gulped down a big sip, choosing to have the mug remain in my hands.

Footsteps shuffled into the kitchen. It was Elena.

"What are you doing here?" I asked.

She scratched the side of her head. "I heard you coming downstairs, and wanted to see if everything was okay."

I put the mug down on the kitchen counter. "I didn't think you still cared."

Elena rolled her eyes. "Don't be stupid."

An uneasy feeling returned to my throat, lingering for a bit. "No matter what you think of me, what happened in Mexico wasn't our fault. It was an accident, and we can't continue to blame ourselves. And also, just for the record, I didn't enjoy killing Paul. For lack of a better excuse, it just happened in the heat of the moment and I'm tired of you making me feel like I'm a bad person."

"I know. I know." Elena opened her arms, inviting me in for a hug.

It was the most cordial we'd been too each other in a while, and it'd be nice if it lasted forever. The world was a scary place. And I needed all the allies I could get.

# Chapter 20

I woke up several mornings later, and found Detective Sanders and Elena's mom standing in the kitchen.

I folded my arms. "What's going on?"

Detective Sanders flashed me a smile, revealing her perfect teeth. At least she had a good dentist. She needed it if she ever hoped at attracting a man someday. "As I was just telling Mrs. Brooks, I have footage, which proves you were never kidnapped."

I raised an eyebrow at her. "What are you talking about?"

Mrs. Brooks coughed into her arm. "It's true. She showed me a copy of it on her iPhone. I'm afraid it doesn't look good, Cassandra. I'm sorry."

"There's nothing to be sorry about." Detective Sanders put her hands in her pockets. "It's the truth. So now you're gonna have to come down to the police station and answer a few questions."

I smirked. "Fine. You can bring me in for questioning all you want. I'll be having Elena's mom here file a lawsuit on my behalf, suing you for police brutality by the end of business today.”

Mrs. Brooks shot me a glance. “I think it’d be best to get it out of the way. Don’t you?”

I exhaled a breath. “Fine. You do have a point. If I go to the police station this instant, it doesn’t have to ruin my entire day.”

Mrs. Brooks put her hand over her head, choosing to remain silent. Even she had her moments when she must have wished I would just hold my tongue. It didn’t matter. Detective Sanders needed to know who she was dealing with. I was Cassandra Fucking Jenkins. Nobody put me down for long—it was a simple law of nature. I survived so much in such a short amount of time. One more thing wasn’t a big deal. I would handle it like a pro.

* * *

Detective Sanders finished playing the video on the TV she wheeled into the interview room. Elena’s mom was also in the room.

She cocked her head to face me. “How do you explain this, Cassandra? This shows you weren’t abducted. You are with Paul in a hotel lobby in Miami?”

I grimaced. “He made me go with him to Miami. It wasn’t like I had a choice. But I think you’re avoiding the more pressing question of how you got this video in the first place.”

She pressed a button on the remote, causing the TV to flash off. “A video was delivered to the police anonymously. And then we verified it with the hotel in question.”

I shifted my gaze to Mrs. Brooks. “Don’t you get it? The police are manufacturing evidence.”

Mrs. Brooks bit her lip. “I don’t know, Cassandra. It looked real to me.”

I stared Detective Sanders down, almost spitting at her. “Are you gonna charge me, or what?”

"No. We don't have enough evidence right now. I consulted the district attorney's office, and she said she's going to need more to proceed." Detective Sanders broke off a piece of her muffin, scarfing it down in a matter of seconds.

I got up, not bothering to push the chair in. "Then we're leaving. I might be a minor. But last time I checked, you can't keep me here if you aren't gonna charge me."

Mrs. Brooks glanced at Detective Sanders, then the bitch nodded.

It wasn't until the clinking sound of the ignition that Mrs. Brooks opened her mouth again. "We need to talk."

I slouched. "Fine. Let's talk. What's on your mind?"

She checked her mirrors before pulling out of the parking lot and plowing down the road. "I have put up with a lot, Cassandra, but that ends today. You are obviously lying to me. So, I'm going to give you one opportunity to tell me the truth."

I glanced out the window while the trees bounced in the background. "I was never kidnapped. Paul helped me fake my kidnapping to escape my abusive father. That's how Lucy and I got our scars. He burned us with cigarettes amongst other things."

Mrs. Brooks remained silent. At least she was smart enough not to interrupt me. I'd give her that much.

"Except I used my father's death as an excuse to come because there was no more reason to be on the run and also because Paul was beginning to be untrustworthy," I said, deciding to reach for a bottle of soda that was in the cup holder before continuing with the rest of my story. "But then Detective Sanders started getting suspicious. It was obvious from the beginning. So, I had Paul come forward to confess the whole thing. But I wasn't about to have him go to jail for a crime he didn't commit so I broke him out of the police station. Trust me. You don't want to ask.

But then I needed him to come back. Detective Sanders was getting more suspicious. I wanted him to turn himself in for real. He wouldn't hear of it. He ended up blackmailing me for money around the time you were out of town, so I stabbed him with a letter opener, and then dragged him to the woods, and drenched his body in gasoline before lighting him on fire."

Mrs. Brooks cried in a such a tone that I couldn't tell if she was mad or sad. "What about Elena, Lucy, Chuck, Dylan and Robbie? Are they involved?"

"No."

"You're meaning to tell me all this was going on and Elena and Lucy didn't hear a thing?" she asked.

I clicked my lips together. "No. They didn't. They were busy with after school activities."

She came to an abrupt halt when we approached a STOP sign. "I don't even know where to start. I guess the first question is why didn't you tell anyone?"

Tears fell down my face. There was nothing I could do—the game was over. It was for real now because whether I wanted to admit it or not, I was gonna have to be honest with Elena's mom, to a point at least. I had to be honest about myself but there was no way I wasn't going to incriminate everyone else. Not now. Too much happened.

"You have no idea what my life was like, Mrs. Brooks," I said, still unable to look her in the eye. "I wanted nothing more than to tell someone but I couldn't."

She made a right turn. "Believe it or not, I understand your situation more than you think I do. But enough about me. We have to figure out a way to keep you out of trouble. I'm not about to let you rot in jail."

I shot her a brief glance. "You don't think I'm a terrible person, do you? You understand I didn't want to kill Paul, right? It's just this whole situation spun out of control, and turned into something unimaginable. And I had to start telling one lie after the next."

She gave me a brief pat on my shoulder. "I know,

dear. You don't owe me any explanations. But don't you worry! We are going to get you out of this situation. I just know it."

Mrs. Brooks and I shared one thing in common. Optimism. It was kind of nice. She hadn't lost touch with reality even though she was an "adult." It was also something more adults could stand to act like.

I ran my fingers through my hair, feeling the greasy texture. The stress of the current situation must have caused me to forget to condition my hair. "Do you think we should sue Detective Sanders for police brutality?"

"Did you make up the story?"

A burning sensation shot through my stomach. "Yes, I did. But you don't understand. I might be a liar, but that bitch still wants to make my life a living hell. I just can't take it anymore. It'd actually be a relief if God struck me dead."

She grunted. "Don't say that, Cassandra. Anyway, getting back to your question, it's up to you. I obviously think you did an immoral thing, but I can understand why you felt the need to do it. The only issue I have is a lawsuit just won't bring unwanted attention to her. It will put you in the spotlight as well. And I'm not sure you want that at the moment."

Whether I realized it or not, she had a point. My need for revenge couldn't trump the need to protect myself. It was a balancing act.

* * *

Chuck, Dylan, Robbie, Lucy, Elena, and I gathered in my bedroom for another impromptu meeting sometime after seven in the evening."

Dylan grinned. "What's going on, Cassandra? Does this have anything to do with why you weren't in school?"

Lucy's eyes bulged. "Did you rat us out? Is that why you talked to Detective Sanders in the park the other day? Are you trying to save yourself?"

I shook my head in a vigorous fashion. "No. I was just trying to blackmail her."

"Maybe we should just let Cassandra speak before we rush to judgment. What do you say?" Elena said.

"Detective Sanders has proof I was never kidnapped. She has video footage of Paul and me from a hotel in Miami, which means she has concrete proof we are connected," I said, making sure to look everyone in the eye.

Lucy scoffed. "You've got to be kidding me. How could you be so reckless?"

I put my hands on my hips. "You're the one who is kidding me, Lucy. I threw myself under a bus. I had to tell Elena's mom everything but I just mentioned myself. Detective Sanders doesn't know about you guys."

Lucy grunted. "It doesn't matter, Cassandra. You still went behind our backs. What were you thinking? Besides, we both know it won't take long for Detective Sanders to connect the dots. It just takes one mistake for everything to fall apart."

Elena glared at Lucy. "We don't know that for sure."

"Anyway," I said. "I just wanted to be honest, and give you and update."

Elena nodded. "Thank you. I think I can speak for everyone when I say we appreciate the update."

Lucy cackled. "Not me. If you want a thank you, then you will be sadly mistaken."

"Also, I think someone is after me because Detective Sanders mentioned someone sent the police the footage." I tugged at the sides of my jacket before my arms fell to my sides.

* * *

I ended up taking a couple of sleeping pills to fall asleep hours later. It wasn't about killing myself or anything—I honestly needed a good rest.

I rubbed my eyes for a second, then glanced around my room. Someone in a gas mask hovered over me. I blinked before rubbing my eyes for a second time. The only problem was knowing if what I saw was real or if it was a side effect from being drowsy.

But whatever the case, one thing was clear.

The hairs on my back didn't rise for no reason.

# Chapter 21

I walked into the kitchen several afternoons later, discovering Elena's mom just emptied the dishwasher.

She grinned. "Hi, dear! I've been meaning to talk to you."

I grabbed the sides of my necklace. "Did I do something wrong?"

Mrs. Brooks whipped her head back and forth. "It's about Detective Sanders."

My eyebrows knitted together. "I don't understand. Does she want me to go in for more questioning?"

"No. I hired a lawyer because I was a little worried about you, and didn't want to see anything bad happen to you. Anyway, the lawyer says there's no active investigation against you in the District Attorney's office."

I gasped. "You lost me."

"Yes. It is initially true they were pursuing your case until Paul left town. But things changed. Detective Sanders has gone rogue," Mrs. Brooks said.

"Why didn't she present the video to the District Attorney's office? It's enough ammunition to bury me." I reached into the cabinet for a glass, deciding to get myself a glass of water.

Mrs. Brooks sighed, causing her chest to jump and down a few times. "Detective Sanders is a little bit of a black sheep in the police department. Ten years ago, she heavily pursued a case against a man who was accused of killing his pregnant wife. It turns out he was innocent. But they didn't discover that till after the trial was over when new DNA evidence came to life. And her reputation never quite recovered even if they didn't fire her."

"Does the lawyer think Detective Sanders gonna continue to build a case against me?" I asked, finishing the rest of my water.

Mrs. Brooks shrugged. "I don't know. Maybe. I must admit that the woman seems disturbed."

I shoved the glass to the side. "Let me get this straight. As far as the police are concerned, Paul just died on the trail behind our house, and they haven't found a way to link me to the crime?"

She nodded. "Yes. That's exactly what I'm saying. But you need to be careful with Detective Sanders. Because I don't mean to be rude or anything, but she isn't exactly your biggest fan."

I laughed. "That's an under-statement."

Wow. Mrs. Brooks actually said it out loud. The District Attorney's didn't have an open file on me. It was nice that my concerns about Detective Sanders were being validated. I couldn't even begin to imagine how that man must have felt—he had it worse than I did. He went to trial whereas I hadn't. Mrs. Brooks was right about one thing. I was gonna have to be more careful now than ever after discovering Detective Sanders had a shady past. It wouldn't be too difficult for her to ruin me. It would still be nice to see her become flabbergasted after presenting an alternative to the crime—it would be worse than her eating something sour. I would crush Detective Sanders. There was no doubt about it. I had something she didn't now. An upper hand. And I would make damn sure I enjoyed every minute of it.

* * *

I met with Detective Sanders in the park a couple of hours later. It couldn't wait. It was time to make that bitch realize once and for all that she was messing with the wrong person.

"What do you want?" Detective Sanders asked.

I repositioned myself on the park bench, making sure I was comfortable. "I know everything, Jane. I know there's no open case file on me in the District Attorney's office. And I also know about your history for going rogue. I guess you wanted to make sure you had everything taken care of before you went to your superiors about your suspicions."

"How did you find out about that?"

"I have my sources."

Detective Sanders remained silent while she tapped her hands on her knees. It was nice know she was on the defensive, and no longer on the offensive. She made my life a nightmare for far too long. Besides, it was also a nice idea to disrespect authority figures. That was the annoying thing about adults. They thought their age was a license to do whatever the fuck they wanted without paying any consequences whatsoever. It was rather nauseating. The world shouldn't be like that, but it was. It would be tolerable though. I was a survivor, which meant I always found a way to get what I wanted.

There was another thing that still had to be dealt with. I had no idea who was walking around in a gas mask costume. A thought formed in my mind, causing me to scratch the side of my head. There was no way it could be true. Detective Sanders might have been crazy, but she didn't have the time to stalk me.

Wait.

Stalk wasn't exactly the right word. But it was the only one I could think of when it came to the gas mask man. The person almost killed me. After all, it wasn't like I could forget about almost being strangled. It was bad enough to be the victim of an act of violence. The fact it happened in my bedroom brought it to a whole new level. It meant the person didn't have any boundaries if they didn't care about hurting me in the privacy of my own home. It was also kind of morbid. If I couldn't be safe in my own home then I was definitely doomed the moment I stepped out of my own home.

Even if Detective Sanders didn't do it, it still didn't hurt to throw around a false accusation.

I swallowed the awkward feeling in my throat, forcing it away. "I know it was you dressed up in a gas mask. I mean, don't you think that's a new low? Strangling me just because I'm forcing you to actually do your job?"

She rolled her eyes. "I have no idea what you're talking about. Perhaps you need professional help. This town has a nice psychiatric hospital. Maybe I could even take you there myself."

I snickered. "You wish."

Detective Sanders got up from the park bench. "I don't have time to waste. Don't call me again unless you want to confess to Paul's murder. But I'd be careful. I can't imagine Paul's mom is too happy that her son's killer walks the street."

She darted away into the opposite direction without another word.

My conversation was still worth a shot even though it hadn't gotten me anywhere. It was nice to know she wasn't the only person who could throw around false accusations. It would have been great to have a voodoo doll of Detective Sanders because if I did, I would stick needles in it all day long without any hesitation.

* * *

I ran into Chuck the following morning in the school parking lot.

"Wait up," I called out to him from a distance.

He whirled his body around to face me. "Hi, Cassandra. What's up?"

I flocked over to him as fast as I could. "Not much. But there is one thing I need to tell you about."

"Everything okay?"

I whipped my head back and forth. "I'm afraid not. Detective Sanders has gone rogue with the police department. Elena's mom's lawyer found out there's no case file on me."

He put a piece of gum in his mouth. "But what about the videotape? I don't understand? No offense or anything, but it doesn't exactly look good for you. Does the lawyer have an explanation for that?"

"She's just waiting to have a tighter case against me, as she has a history of going outside the scope of her authority."

"What are you gonna do?"

I shrugged at him. "I don't know. But whatever I decide, I'm gonna have to make up my mind soon. I'm tired of having this hang over my head. I just want to move on."

"Yeah, I can understand that."

*** 

I decided to use lunch as an opportunity to talk to Lucy as she always goes to her locker before heading to the cafeteria.

I tapped her back.

Lucy turned around, almost melting me with her stare. The peace between the two of us must not have been destined to last long. "What do you want?"

"We need to talk, Lucy. To be honest, it kind of

seems like you're sending mixed signals. One minute things are fine between the two of us. And then the next you're giving me the cold shoulder. What gives?"

She finished zipping up her backpack before glancing back at me. "I realized I'll never be able to trust you."

"I thought things were good between us. Or have you forgotten that I can drag you down to hell with me?"

"Relax, I'm not going to go to Sanders about my suspicions."

I shot her a dirty look. There was just no time to hide my emotions. "I still want to know why you were following me in the first place. I mean you didn't really think I was going to sell you out? Did you?"

She drew in a deep breath. "No. Not at first. But then I realized you are the girl that came up with the kidnapping story. Maybe I was too quick to trust you."

"Fine. Have it your way." I strutted down the hallway. There was no point in continuing my conversation.

Lucy made up her mind about me whether I wanted to admit it or not, and I was going to have to live with that. However, that did mean I had to stand there and take it.

* * *

I knocked on Elena's bedroom hours later sometime in the evening.

"Come in," said the voice behind the door.

I pushed the door open to discover Elena doing homework in her notebook while resting in bed. "Do you have a minute?"

She looked up at me for a moment. "Yeah, of course. Everything okay?"

Phew. For a second, I deluding myself into thinking life was okay, because I had my best friend to chat with. I just didn't know what I would've done if Elena didn't wanna be bothered with me—everyone needed to a confidant at some point. Being a little selfish was only natural, and anyone who refused to acknowledge that fact was lying.

I rubbed the side of my neck. "I've lost Lucy. I mean, I trust her not to rat me out, but there is nothing genuine between us."

"I'm sorry to hear that," she said, pushing a chunk of her hair to the side. "I know how much fixing things with Lucy meant to you."

I exhaled a breath. "It's fine. It's nothing I haven't dealt with before."

"As long as you can live with it."

"There is one good thing that came out of today," I said.

She leaned in a little closer, almost as if her life depended on my response. "And what's that?"

"I'm going to break into Detective Sanders's home, and destroy the video tape of the hotel school security footage."

# Chapter 22

Elena scoffed. "Are you crazy? You just can't break into a detective's house. You could get caught. Besides, what makes you think she even has the videotape in her home."

"It's simple. She probably thinks it's the safest there," I said. "Anyway, you really don't need to worry about me, Elena. I'm not an idiot. I'm going to hack into her security system and disable the alarm for a half an hour."

"Okay." Elena swallowed the lump in her throat. "But how are you going to get into her house without a key?"

I laughed. "I know how to pick a lock, Elena. This isn't my first scheme."

Elena ran her fingers through her hair. "Okay. As long as you know what you're doing then that'll be fine."

"But it's not like Detective Sanders is an innocent—she's ruining my life."

She shifted her attention back to her notebook. "Whatever you say. Anyway, do you know what you'll do about Lucy?"

"I don't know. What do you think I should do?"

"Do you want my honest opinion?" Elena asked.

I nodded. "Yeah. That'd be nice."

"You should leave the situation alone. I know it must be upsetting, but there's nothing you can do at the moment. So, you just have to focus on extracting yourself from the Paul situation."

She did have a point.

My relationship with Lucy couldn't be fixed overnight. It'd take time. The bottom line was having a mended relationship with Lucy wouldn't do me any good if I went to jail.

It didn't matter if breaking into Detective Sanders's house was risky. It was something that had to be done. There was nothing like the mantra, "go big or go home." This wasn't amateur hour, which meant I couldn't just sit back and let my future unfold. I had to take charge of my future no matter how difficult it would be. That was what separated me from the rest of the world. I wasn't afraid to do the things that were necessary whereas other people were too worried about getting their underwear messed up. It was pathetic. Idealism wouldn't save me. Cunning, calculated behavior was the only option. It was a matter of survival, after all.

* * *

I skipped school the following day, and currently stood outside Detective Sanders's front door, attempting to pick the lock. The alarm system had been disabled for two hours, as I wanted to give myself enough time to snoop through her house. Half an hour had been a low estimate.

Someone tapped my back, causing me to whip around.

"What are you doing here, Chuck?" I asked.

He folded his arms. "Elena told me you'd be

here."

"You've gotta get out of here. You can't be here. You aren't even dressed properly. At least I'm wearing a black hooded sweatshirt and black pants."

He averted his gaze, choosing to look at the fallen leaves. "Yeah. I guess I could put a little more thought into things."

The door sprung open a minute later.

I grabbed his arm. "Come on. Let's go inside before anyone sees us."

I released his arm, after which I made sure to shut the door behind us.

"Do you even have any idea where she would keep the video?" he asked.

Sweat crashed down my face, causing me to think about the intensity of the situation even if I didn't want to. "I don't know. Good question. Why don't we try the kitchen first?"

We shuffled through the living room, making our way into the kitchen. The two of us searched through the drawers, unable to find anything.

"Why don't we go upstairs?" I said.

I trekked out of the kitchen, heading towards the stairs. It wasn't long before we ascended the staircase.

We arrived at her bedroom a moment later, discovering a desk. I started opening the drawers, and it wasn't long before something with the label Hotel Footage popped out at me.

I waved the DVD at him. "I have it. Unfortunately, we don't have anything to play the video."

"Good thing I came prepared." He unzipped his backpack, pulling out his laptop.

He rested the laptop down on the table, pulling his hand out at me to give him the DVD. I obliged. Chuck popped the TV into the laptop. It wasn't long before a video appeared and he pressed play. The two of us looked on at the video, realizing it was the same video Detective

Sanders showed me.

I rested my hands on his back. "This is it. We found the video."

Chuck took the DVD out of the laptop, then handed it to me. "Here! You should probably destroy it."

Footsteps scraped the floor, then I peeked out into the hallway—no one was there. It didn't make any sense. Regardless of who had or hadn't been the hairs on my back stood up. A thought formed in my mind, begging the question if it could actually be true. The person in the gas mask couldn't have been in Detective Sanders's house. It didn't make any sense unless the person was stalking me.

I bit my lip.

There was a chance someone might have been stalking me no matter how upsetting it might have been for me to think about. It was obvious even if I didn't have to admit the truth to Detective Sanders. She wasn't the person in the gas mask—I would have bet my life on it. She seemed genuinely surprised when I told her about it. Besides, there was a creepy feeling to the whole gas mask situation because it was kind of thing that required calculated behavior and that was something Detective Sanders didn't have. She was lucky if she knew how to tie her shoes. And no. That wasn't an overstatement. It was the truth. The woman was the most incompetent woman I ever saw.

The footsteps returned, forcing me to put my index finger in front of my mouth while I faced Chuck.

I went back out into the hallway. No one was there. The hairs on my back remained up.

"What's going on?" Chuck whispered while sweat dripped down his face.

"I don't know. But I'm sure it isn't a big deal."

"Really?" His eyebrows danced up his forehead. "It kind of sounds like we aren't alone."

It didn't matter if I was being dishonest. There was no need to worry Chuck. Someone had to protect him since it would too dangerous for him to learn I probably had a stalker even if I couldn't prove it. There was no doubt about it. Although it wasn't easy to admit it was another thing I had to do behind his back. He would understand someday. Just not today. Although if there was anything I learned over the last few months, it was that secrets always came out. It was inevitable—I could at least pretend to play the game a little longer.

* * *

I started a fire in the fireplace hours later when I returned home from my half day of school. I waited a good five minutes for the crackling of red, orange, and yellow to increase in size before throwing the DVD into the fireplace.

It was done.

I would relish my victory even if hubris was a dangerous quality as there hadn't been a lot to be happy about lately. My life seemed like one bad decision after a next and now the bleeding would finally stop. It would have been even funnier if all of the criminals Detective Sanders pursued outwitted her.

"What are you doing?" asked a woman's voice.

I shifted my body, looking the lady right in the eye. "Hi, Mrs. Brooks. Didn't even hear you come in."

She frowned. "Do I even wanna know what you just did?"

"Let's just say I did a good thing. Detective Sanders doesn't have any proof now."

Mrs. Brooks smacked her hand over her mouth after glancing at the fireplace. "Don't tell me you broke into her house to steal the DVD?"

I moved my head back and forth. "I was doing what needed to be done. Don't worry, I wasn't stupid. I disabled the alarm. It really wasn't a big deal."

She put her hand over her head. "I wish you would consult me before doing questionable things."

"Are you angry with me?" I asked.

"No. It just would be nice if you would let me help you. You don't have to be in this alone. I'm here for you."

I forced a grin at Elena's mom. "I know, and I appreciate that. It was just something that needed to be done—it's not a big deal."

* * *

I sat with Robbie and Dylan the following morning at the tables in front of the high school's main entrance.

I elevated an eyebrow. "How have things been between the two of you?"

They both glanced at each other, smiling.

"They've been good," Robbie said. "We're looking forward to going to homecoming together. Hopefully, the school won't make a big deal. Not like were the school's first LGBTQ couple.""

Dylan chuckled. "They shouldn't. Straight people don't have to justify their lives to the rest of the world, so neither should gay or bisexual people."

A bug buzzed by my face, causing me to smack it with my hand.

Dylan shot me a gaze. "Sorry. Didn't mean to preach. It's just something I feel passionately about."

I sighed. "No need to apologize. You know I have your back 100 percent."

There was no hint of insincerity to my comment—Robbie and Dylan deserved to have someone support them. They weren't telling other people how to live their lives. And that was a good thing. But that also meant nobody else should be telling them how to behave.

Robbie sipped of his coffee. "How are things with Detective Sanders?"

I smiled. "Let's just say I took care about the problem."

* * *

I drove home from school hours later, because I was finally able to drive now that I had a license and car. Even if a part of me would never be used to my newfound freedom. Elena's mom bought me a car a couple of weeks ago. It must have slipped my mind. There was a lot to think about, after all.

Paul popped back into my head—the whole thing was surreal. There was no way it could have been real, but it was. Paul was dead and there was nothing anyone could do to change the situation.

I pulled into the driveway, discovering Paul's mom standing in front of the garage. The clinking sound of the ignition halted when I pulled out the key. I grabbed my purse from the floor of the car in front of me since that was where my gun was.

I exited the car, tugging at the strap of my purse. I just had to make sure I had my gun.

I shuffled over to Paul's mom. "What the hell are you doing here?"

Yeah. No apology necessary for the rage shooting through my body. I generally frowned with comparing people to animals, but Paul's mother was starting to resemble a cockroach that would survive a nuclear bomb.

She stomped her feet. "I know you killed my son, you fucking bitch."

My nostrils flared up. "You already told me that, sweetheart. Why don't you come back when you have something new to say?"

The woman cackled. "Detective Sanders has proof of what you did, and you are gonna go to jail."

I whipped my gun out from my purse, putting my fingers on the trigger. "I'll say it one last time. I want you off my property."

She put her hands on her hips. "I'd like to see you try."

I pulled the trigger, hitting the side of the house.

"Have you lost your damn mind? You could have killed me."

My hands remained elevated. It would only take one second to pull the trigger. "That was a warning shot. Next time, I won't miss."

My pulse continued drumming in my ears. I just couldn't shake my adrenaline rush. But perhaps that was okay. If I wanted to feel in control, then I needed to act in control.

# Chapter 23

A screeching sound echoed after I returned home from school. I flocked out of the kitchen, making my way to the front door.

"Hi, Chuck, how are you? Why haven't you returned any of my messages," I asked, opening the front door.

His hands rocked back and forth, making the thick envelope he was carrying pop out at me. "We need to talk."

I furrowed an eyebrow. "Everything okay? You seem upset about something."

Chuck shuffled into the house.

We made our way into the kitchen a couple of moments later. He opened the envelope, shoving the two pieces of papers in my face. "Did you know about this?"

"Know about what?" I took the two papers from him, scanning them. One of the pieces of papers was Chuck's birth certificate and the other was Paul's.

"Please don't stand there and feed me some line of bullshit. I guess I didn't mean as much to you as I originally thought."

My arms fell to my sides while I continued gripping the birth certificate with my right hand. "Why do you have Paul's birth certificate?"

"Someone mailed them to me, but that's only a small matter." His Adam's apple throbbed. "Just look at who is listed as the father on both certificates.

I scanned the birth certificates again, realizing what Chuck was talking about. "You and Paul are half-brothers?"

He folded his arms together. "Did you know that he was my half-brother?"

"No. Of course not. I would never keep something so serious from you. Besides, we have a more pressing problem. Paul's mom showed up here recently, and the only way I got her to leave was to threaten to shoot her."

Chuck gasped. "Are fucking kidding me? Were you really gonna shoot the poor woman?"

I sucked on my teeth. "In case you've forgotten, Paul was the one who was blackmailing me and physically assaulted me. Plus, his mother has been hounding me non-stop."

"You were the one who made him go along with the bogus kidnapping story."

"Are you saying that I deserved what I got? I don't get where is all this anger coming from? Do you seriously think I knew you two were half-brothers? I think we should focus on the more pressing issue. In case you've forgotten, someone tried to strangle me in my bedroom a couple of months ago."

He scoffed. "I wouldn't be surprised if you just made that up."

"Do you even hear what you're saying? Because it's pretty fucking ridiculous. I hope you know that."

"You're only upset because I'm calling you out on your bullshit," he said.

"You knew who I was pretty early on in the relationship. So, if you ask me, that says more about you than me."

I couldn't ignore this mysterious person anymore. Someone sent Detective Sanders video of me and Paul at the hotel in Miami and also tried to strangle me in my bedroom. The only problem was the person seemed to vanish into thin air. It was at that moment, I became sure of one thing. Somebody was determined to witness my demies.

***

Unfortunately for me, I ran into Lucy hours after coming out of the bathroom en route back to my bedroom.

She smirked. "I heard you and Chuck arguing earlier. Do I detect trouble in paradise?"

There it was. The old Lucy. She just had to make some sort of jab at me, because that was who she'd always be.

My eyes widened. "You wish. Anyway, if you know what's good for yourself, you'll stay away from Chuck. I don't want you to sabotage my relationship. Because if you do, I'll drag you right down to Hell with me."

Lucy cackled. "Please. As if you need my help. You'll sabotage your relationship all on your own. It's only a matter of time before Chuck sees you for the fraud you are."

"You're lucky you aren't taller, Lucy. Otherwise I'd suspect you to be the person in the gas mask."

She flipped her hair over her shoulders. "I have no idea what you're talking about."

"Sure, you do," I said. "For all I know, you two are working together."

She laughed again, only this time her tone was louder. "It must have been a real shocker to discover Paul and Chuck are half-brothers."

"It's not my fault they have a loser deadbeat father."

"What are you gonna do when the last straw breaks the camel's back? Chuck was the last person who believed in you."

I placed my hands on my hips. "In case you didn't realize, I have Elena, Robbie, and Dylan."

"Not for long. I'm going to steal them from you."

"Doubtful. You can barely parallel park."

"That's your biggest mistake." Lucy paused for a moment. "You shouldn't underestimate me. I know a lot more than you realize."

Lucy walked down the hallway in the opposite direction.

Wow. I shouldn't have been surprised that peace with Lucy was short lived. We were destined to always be at each other's throats like some sort of Shakespeare drama. We'd sleep when we were dead. I could only wonder if one of us would end up killing the other at some point. Not that I needed to be involved in another murder or anything, as I already had a million and one problems to deal with at the moment and wasn't looking to add another to the list.

* * *

I approached Elena at her locker the following morning at school, flashing a grin. "Do you have a moment to talk? I could use a friend."

Elena craned her neck. "Sure. Is something wrong?"

"Paul and Chuck are half-brothers."

"How is that possible?"

I shrugged. "I don't know. I guess it makes sense. A guy only has to sleep with so many women…"

She twirled a strand of her hair. "Let me guess. Chuck thinks you knew about it?"

"Yeah. But I didn't know about it. I swear it."

Elena patted my shoulder. "Give him a chance, Cassandra. I'm sure he'll eventually come around."

"Not if Paul's mom doesn't kill me first."

"What are you talking about?" Elena asked.

"Never mind! Anyway, I'd appreciate it if you could help defuse the situation and possibly talk to Chuck."

Her jaw shook. "I don't know, Cassandra. That's kind of putting me in an awkward position."

"Please. You're the only friend I have."

"That's not true and you know it. Dylan and Robbie would do anything for you," added Elena.

I sighed. "That is if Lucy doesn't take them away from me first."

She scratched the side of her head. "Okay, fine. I'll talk to Chuck. But that's all I can do, because I can't make any promises."

It didn't even matter if I came off as desperate. It was the truth. Things were spinning out of control faster than I would have liked, and I had to find a way to get back on top. I just had to I couldn't even begin to speculate what would happen if things continued on the current downward trend.

* * *

I walked into my bedroom hours later, clapping my hand over my mouth.

Detective Sanders's body and Paul's mom's body were on my bed with two bullet holes in each of their heads.

I screamed, causing my voice to echo through the entire house.

It couldn't be. Detective Sanders and Paul's mom just couldn't be dead. Life wasn't that easy. If someone gave me a gift, then I was certain that something bad was gonna happen at some point soon—it was an unwritten law of the universe.

Elena's mom came to check why I screamed a moment later. She said we had no choice but to call the police, and I agreed with her despite hating the idea. I needed to be truthful with the police even if I would never be a total believer in honesty. This was the one situation when I had nothing to hide. I came home to find the two corpses on my bed. It was the God's honest truth. But only God and I knew it—I wasn't an idiot. Elena's mom hadn't been careful enough to hide her eye roll.

The police left hours later, telling me not to leave town. Even if I wasn't an official person of interest.

Chuck arrived at my house within half an hour of the police leaving. The two of us were plopped down on the living room couch at the moment.

I forced a polite expression. "Thank you for coming, Chuck. I know things have been tense lately…"

"I only came here to talk so I could break up with you."

No. Chuck couldn't have said what he just had. And my reasoning had nothing to do with being in denial and believing people didn't break up with me, I broke up with them. I just didn't know what I'd do if one more thing went bad. I was only a teenager, and could only take so much—I wasn't a television remote that someone could pop a new battery into when a glitch happened.

"What did you just say?" I demanded.

"You heard me!" he exclaimed. "I'm done with you. You haven't returned my texts all afternoon and then you call hours later to demand I come over."

"Well, I'm sorry if I couldn't cater to your incessant demands, but I was a little busy looking at the two corpses in my bedroom." I put my hands on my lap.

"The fuck you talking about?" Chuck asked.

"Maybe if you weren't so busy being an asshole, then you'd be able to pay attention."

"Did somebody die?"

What a fucking idiot.

But no. I'd just count to ten in my mind. I couldn't be too cruel to Chuck even if I wanted to. He knew almost every damning thing about me, after all.

I coughed into my arm. "Yeah. Two people actually. I found Paul's mom and Detective Sanders dead on my bed. And I think somebody is going to set me up to take the fall for their murder."

# Chapter 24

I strutted into the school hallway the next morning, smirking. It didn't matter if somebody was going to set me up to take the fall for murdering Detective Sanders and Paul's mom. They were dead—it was all that mattered. They were both annoying. I could only hope this murder meant I was in the clear, and I wouldn't have to deal with Paul anymore. It wasn't that unreasonable to ask for a fresh start. There were only so many more sleepless nights I would endure. It wasn't like I was Charles Manson or anything. I killed Paul in self-defense, and Chuck was the one that brought my friends over that night. It wasn't like I wanted to make sure I had people to drag down to hell with me.

I wasn't that evil.

At least not yet.

I would also have to admit I had been a little foolish about the Chuck situation. There was only so long that things would be perfect between us. At least he lasted longer than expected. It was something. But unfortunately for me, Chuck was a variable I couldn't afford, which meant he was almost as bad as Lucy. I would have to figure out what I would do about the two of them. Chuck and Lucy couldn't incriminate me without implicating themselves. The genius was in the details even if I hadn't planned it that way.

It was something else to be glad about.

Although if I were being honest, it wouldn't help me sleep at night. I needed something big to bury the situation once and for all. It was my only way out. I would have to pray someone wasn't setting me up take the fall for the two murders…

Chuck approached me a moment later. "Are you seriously smirking at the two deaths? Do you not have any regard for human life?"

"I'm not doing this here." I grabbed his arm, dragging him into an empty hallway.

He rolled his eyes. "What the hell? I'm not your possession."

"Do you really think I'm glad about the two murders?"

Chuck shook his head. "I don't think it, I know it! It's written all over your face."

I pushed a lock of hair out of the way. "Detective Sanders and Paul's mom were making my life a living hell."

"That doesn't change the fact an innocent man died," Chuck said.

"No offense, Chuck, but you have no idea what you're talking about! And in case you're forgotten you're as much a part of the situation as I am. You're the one that brought my friends into it."

"Yeah, I'm aware of that."

I sneered. "You're just pissed because things aren't going as easily as you wanted them to."

"Wow. Your delusions of grandeur are beyond astonishing."

I lunged forward. "I want to know something.

Were you serious when you said you wanted to end things with me last night?"

"Yeah, I was. I can't do this anymore."

"Well, good." I shot him a dirty look. "I'm tired of being punished for not living up to the person you want me to be."

He crossed his arms. "It's not my fault you can't deal with the truth."

I stroked his chin. "I just hope you realize that you're in it deep with the rest of us, and it would be foolish to rat me out."

Chuck pushed my hand away. "Yes. I'm aware of that. You don't have to play nice with me so I'll be silent. You have my word I'll keep quiet."

I shuffled away from Chuck.

Shit. We were over. It really happened. It hadn't been something in my head. Tears plowed down my face, causing me to wipe my eyes. It wasn't a lie with Chuck. There were some genuine elements even if any positive memory was fleeting. Chuck understood me in ways Paul didn't. And it was something I would never forget.

I bumped into someone a moment later.

"Watch where you're going, bitch," said the person.

I lifted my gaze, realizing who it was. "Maybe you're the one who should be watching where you're going, Lucy."

Lucy continued making eye contact. "Did something happen? Why are you crying?"

I sobbed. "Like you care. You're the one who wants to witness my eternal damnation."

"That's not true, and you know it," Lucy replied. "It doesn't have to be like this."

"Are you kidding me, Lucy? One minute you're hot, and the next your cold. Just make up your mind already because this Dr. Jekyll and Mr. Hyde thing is getting really old."

"What happened?"

Wow. We were actually gonna do this. We were gonna pretend to be sisters who cared about each other, because I still hadn't forgotten about my current tension with Lucy. Only a lobotomy would've allowed for that.

I averted my gaze, glancing at Lucy's new Jimmy Choo shoes. "Chuck and I broke up."

"I'm sorry to hear that—I know he meant a lot to you."

"I'll be watching you closely."

"I don't know what you're talking about. My hands are clean."

I pursed my lips. "I think you sent the two birth certificates to Chuck in order to drive a wedge between the two of us."

"That's ridiculous. Anyway, I'd be careful if I were you. You can't afford to make any more enemies."

"Are you threatening me?" I asked. "Perhaps you need to be reminded of the fact I know you killed our father."

"Please." Lucy snickered. "We both know you would have gone to the police already if you had any intention of using that against me."

"I wouldn't be so sure about that."

It wasn't about being dramatic. Lucy had a lot of nerve. Her split personalities were getting hard to keep track of. It was also another variable I didn't need. I had enough problems as it was. I would also be damned if Lucy's split personality blew up the whole plan. It would only take one bad thing for everything to blow up in our faces. And I wouldn't let that happen. I couldn't. It wasn't an option.

* * *

I arrived at a cafeteria table hours later, and found Robbie and Dylan together. "Do you mind if I join you two?"

Robbie grinned. "Absolutely."

I sat, placing my tray on the table.

Dylan looked up at me. "We've actually been meaning to talk to you. Elena told us about the two homicides."

I snorted. "Please! I can't think about that at the moment."

"Did you kill Detective Sanders and Paul's mom?" Robbie whispered.

"Even I'm not that stupid," I said.

Dylan swallowed a lump in his throat. "Do you have any idea what's going on? Do you think Lucy's gone rouge?"

The matter simmered in my mind for a moment, forcing me to consider the reality of the situation. "No. I don't think Lucy's involved with this."

"Well, that's good." Robbie took a spoonful of his yogurt, shoveling it in his mouth.

"Chuck and I broke up," I blurted. "We're really done."

Dylan sipped his water. "That's awful. I'm sorry to hear that."

Robbie squeezed Dylan's hand. It was nice to see somebody was happy even if it wasn't me.

I huffed out a sigh. "I guess I can be glad I don't have Detective Sanders hovering over me."

"Yeah. It's something," Robbie said.

It didn't take a genius to hear Robbie's less than enthusiastic tone in his voice. Problems were like Greek mythology monsters—you cut off one head only to have ten more grow back.

It was a tragedy.

But I didn't have time to cry about anything. I would risk falling even more behind with the situation and that was one reality I was not prepared to deal with him. I couldn't. I wouldn't. My dysfunctional past didn't have to define my future. I deserved a fresh start even if I couldn't admit it out loud.

I glanced at Robbie and Dylan. "But there's one thing we can't waver on."

"And what is that?" Robbie asked.

I popped off the top button of my jacket. "You guys can't ice Chuck out just because we're no longer dating. He might've promised to keep the situation a secret, but we can't taunt him."

"Are you saying we should fake being friends with him?" Dylan devoured the rest of his sandwich.

"No. Just talk to Chuck as if we were still dating. I can't afford a vengeful twin sister and an angry ex-boyfriend at the same time," I said.

Robbie and Dylan nodded, then I breathed a sigh of relief. Their cooperation couldn't be dismissed no matter how mundane it seemed. For once, something went right. And I'd hold onto said fact as long as I could. No telling when the next tragedy would happen.

# Chapter 25

I shuffled over to Chuck one morning at school several weeks later.

He whirled around after I tapped his shoulder. "What do you want?"

I feigned a smile. "We still have things to discuss even if we're no longer together."

Chuck wove his arms together. "I have nothing to say to you."

"You're still an accessory to murder in case you've forgotten."

He tugged at the straps of his backpack, pulling tighter. "Just tell me what you want. You've already wasted enough of my morning as it is."

"Elena's parents are going away on a business conference for the weekend, and I thought that'd be a good opportunity to go to Robbie's lake house." I rubbed the side of my head.

"You can't stop using people, can you?"

"Shut up and listen!" I paused for a moment—no matter how much Chuck's attitude stung, I still couldn't alienate him—only a fool would've done so. "I want to get everyone up to speed about the gas mask situation."

Chuck rolled his eyes. "You seriously can't still be convinced that someone is after you? I mean, the police don't even consider you a suspect in the double homicide."

"That's because I have nothing to hide."

He shook his head. "Well, so you claim…"

"Somebody's bitter about the breakup."

He remained silent. He must not have been able to come up with a good enough comeback. Whatever. Sucked to be him.

"Anyway, just be at Elena's house after school tomorrow. Otherwise I'll send the police an anonymous tip implicating you in Paul's death," I continued.

He smirked. "It's good to know I meant so much to you."

It was a shame things had to be toxic with Chuck. I didn't want it to be like that—it was the truth. Even I wasn't stupid to play a game of chicken with someone who was complicit in helping me cover up a murder.

Murder.

It didn't sound like the right word to describe what happened to Paul even if it was. The image of his corpse would always be burned in my brain no matter how much time went by. There was no debate about it. Seeing both Paul's mom's corpse and Detective Sanders's body would also be forever engrained in my mind. It wasn't something I could just forget. There was nothing like seeing a dead body to shake me to my core.

* * *

Elena and I walked to first period together a few minutes later.

I turned my head. "I got Chuck to agree to go with us this weekend."

Elena exhaled a long breath. "I still don't understand why you want to go away to Robbie's lake house."

I tossed my hair behind my neck with one jerk of my head. "I already told you, Elena There are some things we need to discuss."

She narrowed her focus on me. "Is this about the recent murders?"

Creepy. It was as if Elena read my mind. Perhaps she had a future as a psychic. There were worse professions, after all.

I nodded. "Something like that."

She couldn't suppress her emotions. Laughter reigned from her mouth. "We should just be lucky my mom trusts us to be by ourselves over the weekend."

"And I still can't believe she's kept our secret from your dad."

"No offense to my dad, but he doesn't need to know about the Paul situation."

"Yes. I would have to agree with you with that one."

The two of us turned a corner in the hallway, then made a right. And I even had jealousy pangs from the group of girls engrossed in conversation that Elena and I just walked by. In my mind, they had a perfect life, and that was something to be irked by. I deserved a small amount of happiness—I was only 17 once.

"How are you feeling about Chuck?" Elena asked.

I shifted my attention to one of the winter formal dance posters. "I'm fine. But thanks for asking."

There was nothing like a poster to get somebody to have school spirit. Whatever. Before I knew it, high school wouldn't even be a blimp in my rearview mirror. And I wouldn't have it any other way. I couldn't be shackled to some lame town for the rest of my life. I would rather take arsenic.

She grabbed my arm. "You don't have to put up a front with me, Cassandra. It's obvious you're hurting."

"What am I supposed to say?" I spat. "Do you

want to tell me that it kills me that I wrecked my only honest relationship? Because it does."

Elena put her hair up in a ponytail. "I guess I shouldn't have asked."

"You think."

Elena's efforts were futile even if she meant well. There was no point in talking about Chuck anymore—we were over. It didn't even matter if I wished I could shove my pride aside and give him a real apology. I would never be able to do that, and it was another reality I had to live with.

She glanced at me for a brief moment. "I guess I should be glad you're pretending your relationship with Chuck wasn't real. Anyway, I take it you'll supply the weekend alcohol by using one of your fake I.D.s at the liquor store?"

I gave her a weak smile. "You know me all too well, Elena."

* * *

The trip to the lake house arrived faster than I imagined.

We all met at my house, and Robbie ended agreeing to drive us. We were all able to pile into his minivan. Lucy was even there, because I didn't have to remind her she was in it with the rest of us. Being alone in an empty house must not have been an appealing though, especially since it was the sight of a recent crime scene.

We sat on the floor of the living room hours later, drinking from our red cups.

Elena threw a gaze at me. "Spill it, Cassandra. Why did you want to get away for the weekend?"

"Someone is after me." I sipped my cocktail, chugging down half of it.

Dylan raised an eyebrow. "You couldn't have told us this back home?"

"It wasn't just at the party when someone tried to

strangle me." I glanced down at the wooden floor. "Someone broke into my bedroom over the last couple of months. I'm sure of it."

"And what makes you say that?" Chuck asked.

I put my cup on the floor, deciding to grope through my jacket pocket. I pulled something out a moment later, shaking it at everyone. "I found this watch on the floor of my bedroom, and it doesn't belong to any of us, or Elena's parents," I said.

Yeah. My bad. I was once again guilty of omitting something, in this case, that meant the watch in my bedroom. Whatever. Better to learn about the lie of omission now than later.

Chuck whipped his head back and forth. "It could've been someone at the party."

"This was after the party when I took some sleeping pills. At first, I wasn't sure, but now I am. The person was wearing a gas mask like the man that tried to strangle me." I reached for my red cup, finishing the rest of my tequila and tonic.

Dylan sighed. "Do you think the person also killed Paul's mom and Detective Sanders?"

"Yeah, I do. I don't think it's that much of a leap," I said.

Elena fanned herself with the collar of her shirt while sweat continued crashing down her face. "Do you think you're gonna be framed for murder, Cassandra?"

I shrugged. "I don't know, maybe. Although I appear to be in the clear so far. But it's too much to be a coincidence. We also can't forget about my blackmail note upon my homecoming. And the security footage that was sent to Detective Sanders."

Lucky cackled, rattling the air with her voice. "I was the one who sent you the blackmail note in case you couldn't figure it out."

I stared my sister down. "You can't be serious. You didn't really send me the note, did you?"

Her smile widened, giving her another opportunity to show off her blinding, white teeth. "Yeah, I did."

I got up from the floor, pointing my index finger at her. "Are you kidding me? You're the one who set fire to our house and murdered our father. I mean, did you even stop to think that there might have been things I wanted in the house?"

Chuck, Elena, Robbie, and Dylan exchanged glances

Lucy sneered. "Have you lost your mind? There's nothing in that house worth remembering."

"Did you send the hotel footage to Detective Sanders?" I asked.

Lucy stood, then dusted herself off. "No, I didn't. I only sent you the blackmail note. But it's not like I even did anything about it."

"You know who the man in the gas mask is, don't you?" I demanded.

"No, I don't. I swear it," Lucy said.

"I don't believe you!" I screamed, causing my voice to echo through the living room. "You know what? Get the hell out of here! Nobody wants you here. You're dead to me. Do you understand?"

Lucy sobbed, and for a split second, I almost believed her. "You can't just say that—we're sisters. Does that mean anything to you?"

I snorted. "Well, I guess it meant nothing to you because you blackmailed me."

"Besides," Lucy said. "I helped you all cover up a murder. Like you said, Cassandra. We can't turn our backs on each other. We're all bound together whether we like it or not."

# Chapter 26

I ran out of the house, making my way to the beach sometime later.

The wind whistled, causing the trees to sway back and forth. I fought back the tears. I couldn't cry about Lucy—her betrayal shouldn't have shocked me. She made her feelings clear ages ago, and I was too stupid to realize she didn't want anything to do with me.

I sat on the beach, realizing I still didn't know who the man in the gas mask was.

The hairs on my back pricked up when someone patted me. I shifted body, discovering who it was. "What do you want, Chuck? Because I don't feel like arguing at the moment."

He sat next to me. "I didn't follow you out here to argue. I just wanted to make sure you were okay."

I forced a smile. "You don't have to pretend to be the nice ex-boyfriend."

"I'm not." Chuck swallowed a lump in his throat. "I really do care about you even if we aren't dating any-more."

"Yeah, me too. It's a shame things didn't work out differently."

He jabbed my shoulder. "Maybe we were a little hasty about breaking up."

I exhaled a breath. "No. I want you to be with me because you want to, not because we're bound together for life for covering up a murder. Although I do want you to know one thing."

"What would that be?" Chuck asked.

I didn't even wince. "I didn't enjoy killing Paul."

"I know, I know. I suppose I owe you an apology."

"What do you have to be sorry about? You're the one who put up with my crap."

He inhaled a breath. "I know. But that still doesn't change how I have no idea what your life was like."

"Do you think it was all a lie with Lucy?"

"I don't know…"

I squeezed his hand. "I just want you to know I didn't make it up. She really set the fire that killed my father."

He continued holding my hand. "I believe you, Cassandra. You don't owe me any explanations."

"You just don't know what it was like, Chuck. Everything just spiraled out of control and each lie fed the next."

He let go of my hand. "You didn't have to have everyone continue to be nice to me after we ended things."

I looked away from him, choosing to focus on the chaotic nature of the waves crashing into the beach. "I don't know how much longer I can keep doing this, Chuck."

His eyes bulged up. "You aren't thinking of killing yourself, are you?"

An uneasy feeling returned to my throat. "You said it, I didn't."

He stared me down. "Look, I'm sorry things aren't going well but you can't guilt me into getting back with you."

I glared at him. "What makes you even think I want to get back together with you? That's kind of conceded, don't you think?"

"Sorry. I should've known better."

It didn't even matter if I wanted to get back together with Chuck. I refused to let him know that. I couldn't let him think I'd just run back to him on a whim. He needed to know I was a strong person. He was the one who would have been lucky to have me. Although it was still nice he was at least considering the possibility of getting back together. It was something to be glad about. Chuck was the best thing that ever happened to me. I could never admit it out loud to him though. He just couldn't know he had that much influence over me. I also refused to be vulnerable with another human being. There was only so many beat downs one person could take.

I'd get back together with Chuck someday—just not today. The thought of dying alone was just that nauseating. Being with Chuck wasn't settling. He was a nice person, and aside from our one major argument, he treated much better than Paul had. At least with Chuck, I didn't have to be worried about my physical safety—it was a luxury I needed despite being hard to come by. My emotional safety was also important. But that was a problem for another time, as I didn't have time to be weighed down by my feelings. It wasn't about being mean. It was just another unfortunate thing that became true about my life whether I wanted it to be or not.

"Can we please talk?" called out a voice.

I rose. "I have nothing to say to you, Lucy."

Lucy hung her head lower. "You have to believe me. It was just a stupid prank—I never meant to hurt you."

"How do you expect me to believe you? Besides, it's kind of obvious you're just trying to save yourself," I said.

Her jaw shook. "But I can help you, Cassandra. I think I have an idea who gas mask is."

I raised my hand at her. "No offense, but I'm not interested. Because you could be gas mask, and just be wearing big shoes to fool me."

Lucy scoffed. "You couldn't be further from the truth. If you would just put your ego aside for one moment, you'd realize we were on the same team."

"Funny." I laughed at her comment. "I don't recall wanting someone who stabs me in the back to be on the same team as me."

Lucy and I were two of a kind, which meant she forgot I knew all of her moves. I could spot her insincerity from a mile away.

* * *

I descended the stairwell the following morning, finding everyone in the kitchen.

"Hi!" I exclaimed. "How did everyone sleep?"

Elena shrugged. "Okay. What about you?"

"Fine. But I've actually been up for a little while," I stammered.

Robbie glanced at me. "And it just took you till now to come find us?"

"That's because I was looking for Lucy," I revealed. "I've searched the entire house and property, but I can't find her anywhere. Also, her bed hasn't been slept in. She's gone, and I think something happened to her."

Yeah. Even I couldn't lie to myself this time. Life was about to get more fucked up whether I liked it or not. Because I had no fucking clue where Lucy could be.

# Chapter 27

obbie's gaze constricted. "What do you think happened to her?"

I bit my lip. "I don't know. But it's odd she disappeared without a trace. I really think something is up."

"I'm sure she'll come back soon. She doesn't strike me as having a flight response." Elena grabbed her mug, downing more of her coffee.

My heart fluttered, getting louder with each passing moment. "That's exactly my point. Lucy wouldn't just vanish. She would rather have it out with me than retreat or call it a duel."

Dylan pursed his lips. "Should we call Elena's parents? With everything going on, maybe we shouldn't take any chances."

Robbie shot Dylan a look. "Do you really think the same person who killed Paul's mom and Detective Sanders kidnapped Lucy?"

I nodded. "Yes. I do. I don't think it's a coincidence. Somebody is after me."

Chuck sighed. "How do we know that Lucy isn't behind everything?"

"Because she isn't smart enough to pull something like that off. She's been on edge ever since she killed our father," I said.

Elena shuffled over to me, then gave me a quick hug. "Let's not worry until we have to."

I shoved Elena off me. "I just need to think."

I walked to the glass door, opening it up. Then, I shuffled to the dock.

I glanced up at the sky for a moment. There wasn't a hint of white in the sky. It was kind of ironic. A beautiful day was the backdrop for something dark and twisted.

A bird chirped before flying away from a nearby tree, and it was soon out of sight.

Someone patted my back. "How are you doing?"

I whipped around. "Look, Chuck, I'm not in the mood to talk. Especially with you."

"I'm sure Lucy is okay. There's no reason for you to worry."

"I just feel awful about the way I left things with her last night."

"Worrying isn't going to get you anywhere. I hope you know that," Chuck said.

Chuck had a point even if I didn't want to admit it. There was nothing I could do about Lucy, at least for the moment, that was. She had to be okay. I wouldn't be able to live with myself if something bad happened to Lucy—we were still family even if we fought every other second.

I was sure about one thing, though, despite the confusing turn of events. Lucy wasn't capable of sending the hotel footage to Detective Sanders, and murdering her and Paul's mom. Lucy would have just stabbed me if she had a problem with me.

Chuck stared at me. "What are you thinking

about? You can talk about it if you want."

I tucked a lock of hair to the side. "No. It's fine. I'll just make myself a cocktail."

He wiggled an eyebrow at me. "It's not even ten o'clock in the morning."

"So?" I asked. "It's the weekend. People drink at lunch."

"Whatever! I'm going to pretend I didn't hear that. I just wanted you to know I really am here for you if you need somebody."

"Thanks. I appreciate that."

He sucked in a breath. "Anyway, I don't mean to be rude or anything, but I think we should talk about us."

I tugged at the sides of my jacket. "I can't do this right now, Chuck."

Chuck stroked my chin. "I know you want to get back together with me, Cassandra."

"You're the one who wanted to end things. It's not my fault if you don't know what you want."

He pulled his hand away. "We're never going to figure anything out if we don't discuss our feelings."

I could have gotten everything I wanted, yet I didn't. It wasn't even about self-sabotaging myself. Lucy was my only priority at the moment, and that was the way it had to be. I was 99 percent sure she would do the same thing for me if situations were reversed—at least I hoped so.

That was the funny thing about family. Lucy and I might always be at each other's throats, but loyalty would always be offered without any hesitation.

I frowned. "I don't even know if my sister cares about me half the time, and you have no idea how that feels."

"Yeah, I'm sure that can't be easy."

I pulled Chuck in for a kiss, making sure to give him tongue. Then, he placed his hands on my cheeks.

I pulled back a moment later. "I'm so sorry—I

shouldn't have done that. I wasn't trying to lead you on, I swear it."

It appeared Lucy wasn't the only person I couldn't escape. My fate was also intertwined with Chuck whether I had the courage to admit it or not. And that was okay. Chuck was my epic love, not Paul. And that was the way it was meant to be. He accepted my dark side no matter how many times we fought, and that was something to be glad about it.

* * *

I woke up hours later with a throbbing ache jolting my head.

I rubbed both of my eyes while I kept turning my head, taking in the whole room. I wasn't at the lake house anymore.

I ran over to the light switch—nothing happened after I flicked the switch up. In fact, the darkness would have engulfed me if it weren't for the beams of sunlight sneaking in the room.

My stomach twisted in ten different directions. I scratched the side of my head, realizing someone must have drugged me.

I ran over to the door, then tried opening it. It wouldn't budge. Somebody must have locked it from the outside.

I had no choice but to admit the truth no matter how unpleasant doing so was. I was trapped.

# Chapter 28

I grunted. It didn't make any sense. I couldn't imagine why anyone would want to drug me, and lock me inside some room. It must have been a powerful sedative if I had been out cold for hours. My teeth jabbed my lip. It had to have been the man in the gas mask. He killed Paul's mom and Detective Sanders, possibly kidnapped Lucy, and was probably going to kill me.

I had to get out of here—I couldn't be trapped inside some mysterious room. More sweat fell down my face. It must've been the side effects from being drugged.

I walked over to the closet, rummaging through the items. Then, I smiled when an axe caught my attention from the corner of my eye.

I grabbed the axe, then ripped it through the door. I stepped through the door after opening enough of it to form an exit.

I scanned the hallway for a moment, realizing there was nobody or nothing around. And I took the axe with me. Worrying about self-defense wasn't a bad idea when I had no idea what would happen next.

I came to an empty room a few minutes later, noticing the back of what appeared to be Lucy's head. After that, I ran over to the room. The hairs on my back remained up, though. There was something uneasy about being in a place without any electricity, meaning the house must have been a foreclosure or somebody must have forgotten to pay the electricity bill.

I smiled after realizing I was right. "It's so great to see you, Lucy. You have no idea how worried I've been."

She didn't say anything.

I tapped her neck, causing her head to roll to the floor. I clapped my hand over my mouth, muffling my screams. Lucy was dead. Somebody decapitated her, and then put her hand back on her neck carefully enough to make it look like it was still attached to her body.

It was something from a Stephen King novel.

Wow. Everything with Lucy was over. She was dead, and there wasn't a thing I could do to bring her back. It was beyond tragic. Lucy didn't have to be killed, but she was. And it was just another thing I was going to have to get used to. There would be no opportunities for apologies and reconciliations. We died hating each other, and I was gonna have to live with that for the rest of my life. Wow. Just when I thought life couldn't get more fucked up, it did.

I ran out of the room, gripping the axe even tighter. An icy feeling rubbed up against my back, causing me to turn around. The gas mask man was standing less than ten feet away from me.

I ran as fast as I could, yelling in a tone that I never spoke in before. Then, I turned the corner in the hallway, plowing down the next bit of the hallway. I looked over my shoulder after another beat. Phew. The gas mask man was out of sight.

Someone pulled me into another empty room a moment later. Then, someone shut the door behind me.

I threw a glance at Robbie. "What the fuck is going on?"

Elena coughed into her arm. "We think somebody drugged us. The last thing we remember is having cocktails yesterday afternoon and then bam. We woke up here in some basement."

Dylan's jaw twitched. "Did you find Lucy?"

I swallowed the burning sensation in my throat. "Yeah, I did—she's dead. Someone decapitated her, and placed her head back on her neck and it went flying when I gave her a pat."

Chuck wrinkled his nose. "I'm so sorry, Cassandra."

Elena exhaled a long breath. "There's something you need to see, Cassandra. It's about your mother."

Elena grabbed my hand, guiding me to the back of the room.

I shook my head back and forth. "I don't understand. Why are there photos of my mom here?"

"There's something else. You need to see your mom's death certificate." Chuck handed me a piece of paper. "Look at the time and date of death."

I studied the death certificate for a moment. "What? This can't be? The date is the same day as Lucy and I were born, and the time of death is within an hour after our birth."

Chuck patted my back. "That's not all, Cassandra. We think your father survived the fire, and he is the gas mask man. It's the only thing that makes sense. It'd explain why he physically abused you and Lucy. He was furious your mom died after you two were born. The shrine supports it—he's obsessed with your mom."

I grabbed my neck. "What? He killed Lucy, and now he's gonna kill me?"

Elena sighed. "I'm so sorry, Cassandra."

I shrugged. "I don't understand. Why did he kill Detective Sanders and Paul's mom? It doesn't make sense."

Footsteps scurried in the hallway, making us look at each other.

Robbie's mouth gaped. "We have to get out of here."

Dylan rolled his eyes. "We can't. The window won't budge, remember?"

"Leave that to me!" I walked to the end of the room, gripping the axe tighter. I smashed it through the window, shattering the glass in an instant.

The footsteps grew louder.

"Come on! We have to leave now!" I exclaimed.

Elena nodded. "Cassandra's right. We're better off out there then stuck in this place."

We ran up to the window, then climbed out one by one. Lucky for us, the shattered part of the window was big enough for us to crawl through.

I was the last one out. Unfortunately for me, though, the footsteps were even louder now. The door then opened, and I was almost outside when someone yanked my ankle. I moved my ankle backwards, smacking the person in the head. Robbie and Dylan pulled me out, then Chuck hugged me after I stood.

I glanced up at the house, realizing we'd been held captive in a mansion. It was kind of funny we had been held hostage in a mansion. Almost as if the mansion created a paradox. Something so beautiful—like a mansion—shouldn't have been the setting for something so morbid.

I screamed, then the birds flew out of the trees.

The five of us were still stuck in the middle of nowhere even if we were technically free. The fact was, we had no clue about how to get back home in addition to how my father might've been lurking nearby, preparing to kill me the first opportunity he got.

Yeah. My life was definitely ripped out of a Stephen King novel or some horror movie. And there wasn't a damn thing I could do about it. For the moment, at least.

*Other titles by the authors that you may enjoy:*

## Burning Bridges
## By Chris Bedell

*They've always said that three's a crowd...*

24-year-old Sasha didn't anticipate her identical twin Riley killing herself upon their reconciliation after years of estrangement. But Sasha senses an opportunity and assumes Riley's identity so she can escape her old life.

Playing Riley isn't without complications, though. Riley's had a strained relationship with her wife and stepson so Sasha must do whatever she can to make her newfound family love and accept her. If Sasha's arrangement ends, then she'll have nothing protecting her from her past. However, when one of Sasha's former clients tracks her down, Sasha must choose between her new life and the only person who cared about her.

But things are about to become even more complicated, as a third sister, Katrina, enters the scene...

**Cousin Dearest
By Chris Bedell**

17-year-old Casey has opinions about everything. Like how his grandmother could have been a soap opera actress in another life. And his rantings only increase when his grandma is murdered the night of her 60th birthday party.

Casey must also deal with his budding romance with the next-door neighbor, Logan. However, Logan's mother disapproves of their relationship because of Casey's grandmother being murdered. Disapproval be damned, though. Casey and Logan date despite Logan's mother's initial skepticism.

If life weren't complicated enough, Casey and Logan work together to investigate who killed Casey's grandma. But the killer is watching Casey and Logan. So, Casey and Logan must act quickly if they want to solve the case. If they don't, Casey and Logan might die next.

## I Know Where the Bodies are Buried
## By Chris Bedell

17-year-old Carson believes his former "boyfriend," Billy, didn't commit suicide by jumping off a cliff and into the ocean. Billy's sweater and suicide note might've been found, yet a body was never discovered.

So, Carson befriends, and "dates" his classmate, Dean, on the possibility that Dean knows something about Billy's death. Dean and Billy both belonged to the same community service club (Charity Now) where Billy devoted his time to.

Clues soon unravel, though. Like an eyewitness seeing members of Charity Now in the woods near the cliff before Billy's suicide, a diary entry, proving Billy lied about his father being homophobic, and a hazing incident involving a student's death—that Billy might or might not have been responsible for. However, Carson doesn't only have to grapple with Billy's duplicity. Genuine romantic feelings for Dean emerge. Except Carson will have to finish his sleuthing if he wants closure about Billy's death.

## Soul of a Vampire
## By Silencio Marquez

Kris Kellman is a vampire living in Calgary, Canada who works as a detective at the Magical Laws Division. It's his job to solve crimes committed by magical people like himself. When his former lover, Zeke Yonah, shows up on his doorstep covered in blood and asking for help, Kris is conflicted. Is he a vampire first, or is he a cop?

As he begins to investigate the murder that Zeke doesn't remember committing, things get really complicated when Kris realizes that Zeke is being set up for murder.

Charles Anderson is in charge of the vampire community, and he has a plan to enslave all mankind. The only thing standing in his way are people like Zeke and Kris, a vampire whose loyalty can't be bought. Kris's ridiculous dragon-shifter boyfriend isn't making things easier either.

Kris realizes that if he can't stop Charles, it will mean war between humans and vampires. He knows that it's not just humans that will suffer, but vampires like him who won't just sit by and let Charles get away with genocide.

## Diary of a Vigilante
## By Shaun Curtis

**One man's angel is another man's devil. One man's hero is another man's killer.**

It's a blurred line between hero and villain, between vigilante and criminal, between decent citizen and maniac - and this is where Jack finds himself.

When his friend's family find themselves threatened by a sexual predator and let down by the police, Jack snaps, and a journey of vigilantism, anger and revenge pursues. Told from his point of view, the **Diary of a Vigilante**, Jack descends further into the pits of the underworld, and the man who set out to clean the streets, finds that *he* becomes the top target of law enforcement.

What price will Jack pay for his vengeance, and in a world of eye-for-an-eye justice, what sort of man will he be at the end? Will he become the very same monster he sought to destroy?

## Arc City Stories
## By various authors

*Welcome to Arc City.*

A city that exists in a world beyond governments, where war and climate change have destroyed the old order. Corporations are now the authorities of the surviving city states. The elite live in luxury above the clouds in their towers, everyone else lives further down, based on their corporate and economic worth.

*Arc City Stories* is an exciting, action-packed collection of nine cyberpunk tales, written by eight authors, of various citizens each trying to survive, in their own way, this brave new world.

## A Storm of Magic
## By Ashley Laino

Being brought back from the dead is an impressive trick, even for magician Darien Burron. Now he must try and use his sleight of hand to swindle modern-day witch, Mirah, to sign her power away, or end up a tormented demon in the afterlife.

Meanwhile, sixteen-year-old Mirah is starting to lose control of her powers. After an incident at her aunt's Witchery store, Mirah is sent to a secret coven to learn to control her abilities.

While away, Mirah meets up with a soft-spoken clairvoyant, a brazen storm witch, and the creator of dark magic itself. The young woman must learn to trust in herself before she loses herself entirely to the darkness that hunts her.

## Consumed
## By Justin Alcala

Sergeant Nathaniel Brannick is trapped in Victorian London during a period of disease, crime, and insatiable vices. One night, Brannick returns from work to find an eerie messenger in his flat who warns him of dark things to come.

When his next case involves a victim who suffered from consumption, he uncovers clues that lead him to believe the messenger's warning. Despite his incredulity, he can't help but wonder if the practical man he once was has been altered by an investigation encompassed in the paranormal. That is, until he meets the witch hunters, and everything takes a turn for the worse.

www.blkdogpublishing.com

www.ingramcontent.com/pod-product-compliance
Lightning Source LLC
Chambersburg PA
CBHW012014050726

47590CB00009B/3177